Also By Lisa Stanbridge

Abandoned Hearts

Navigate to the link below to read more about her books.

https://lisastanbridge.wixsite.com/lisastanbridgeauthor/books

Lonely in Paris

Longing for Home Book 1

Lisa Stanbridge

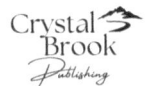

LONELY IN PARIS

Copyright © 2023 by Lisa Stanbridge

The moral right of the author has been asserted

ISBN: 978-0-6456673-0-1

For Pete – the love of my life.

Chapter 1

Jane

My boss assured me that Paris was "the City of Love." That I would *love* living there and I wouldn't miss life in Australia.

She was wrong.

I've never been so lonely.

Three months into a six-month contract and I'm already counting down every second until I fly home.

Thirteen weeks—

I glance at my watch and work it out in my head.

Ten hours, thirty minutes, and...twenty-eight seconds until take-off.

Told you. I'm counting.

"*Cappuccino pour Jane!*"

"*Merci beaucoup.*" I smile and step forward to take the cup.

The barista doesn't notice me, too busy making coffee for the next waiting customer. With a sigh, I turn and leave the café with my head down. I step outside onto the cobblestone pavement, the cool springtime air hitting my face like sharp needles. Not watching where

I'm going, I run into a hard chest and shriek. The impact makes me squeeze the disposable cup, and the lid pops off, coffee splashing all over me and the other person.

I gasp as the cup slips from my hand, falling to the ground next to the lid. "I'm so sorry!" Then remembering I'm in Paris and should be speaking French, I clumsily repeat it. "Uh, *je suis vraiment désolé.*"

I hold my arms out wide, coffee soaking into my white blouse and navy-blue skirt. One glance at the poor victim, a man in his early thirties, shows he's as shellshocked as I am. He looks at his coffee-stained suit, then at me, before starting to rant in French, gesticulating wildly at his suit, which is well cut, tailored no doubt, and his exquisite shoes. In one word: expensive.

Only snippets of what he's saying make sense: "careless," "expensive," "no time,"...you get the gist. He's annoyed.

"Uh, *s'il vous plaît.*" Flustered, I dig around in my bag. "Um, *laissez-moi*, uh, help—"

Ugh. I suck at French so bad. Cheeks burning, I grab the first thing I can find to placate him and hold it out. A lone tissue. He stops mid-rant and looks at it, then at me, before he flicks it away. It flutters to the ground next to the lid and cup, soaking into the spilt coffee.

Yeah, like one tissue would solve our problem.

"Do you speak English?" I desperately ask, hoping to resolve this in a language I'm confident speaking. If I dare try to pacify him in French anymore, I'll probably end up calling him an elephant, or worse. I've improved over the last three months, but I still struggle to hold a conversation.

The man rolls his eyes but nods. "*Oui*, I speak a little English."

Well, this is a good start. "Sir, I'm truly sorry. How can I make it up to you?"

He glares at me, deadpan. It's unnerving that he's clearly annoyed, but he's also in no hurry to move. People are pushing past us to get in and out of the café, but neither of us moves.

"Uh," I look around frantically, "can I buy you a coffee?"

A single eyebrow raises this time, and I bite my lip. "Yeah, bad idea, I agree." I giggle nervously and touch my fingers to my lips. "Uh, how about I pay for dry cleaning?"

His face softens, and this time he attempts a small smile. The tension between us dissipates, and my shoulders slacken.

He nods once. "*D'accord*, you pay for dry cleaning." His French accent is strong, but I understand him. "This is a very expensive suit, *non*?"

I narrow my eyes. Well, I *thought* I understood him. "Uh, it's not?"

His eyebrows knit together in confusion, which in turn makes me confused. Then I realise what he means. "Oh, I understand, you mean it *is* expensive."

That deadpan look returns. "*Oui*, that is what I said. My English is not good."

I rub my lips together and shrug one shoulder. "It's okay, my French isn't very good, either."

He shakes his head, but amusement dances in his dark gaze. "Your French is *very* bad. You insult the entire country of France."

"Hey, it's not *that* bad!"

This time he raises both eyebrows, and I laugh despite myself. Of course, he's right.

"All right, all right, I'll give you that one."

He smiles a real smile this time, revealing dimples in both of his cheeks. The dimples alone make me weak at the knees. He's handsome, I decide. Square face with a sharp jawline and angled cheekbones, chocolate-brown eyes that crinkle at the sides when he smiles, and thick, coiffed brown hair. He's tall, about six feet, and I'm only a couple of inches shorter. Such a nice change to meet a man taller than me, as most of my friends, and even my ex, are shorter.

To formalise our meeting and hopefully leave on amicable terms, I hold out my hand. "I'm Jane, Jane Collins."

He takes my hand, which fits snugly in his warm grasp, and holds it firmly, giving it a shake. A jolt of electricity shoots up my arm, an unexpected ripple dancing down my spine. Our gazes clash, and I drown in his warm brown eyes, inquisitive yet oddly cautious. My breath catches and my body vibrates. Who *is* this man?

He's the first to pull back, and a shutter comes down over his features. "You have a *fade* name." His brow furrows. "I do not know English word."

Fade? I cock my head to the side. What's that word in Eng—

I gasp. "My name is *not* bland!" And just like that, I crash down to earth, feeling slightly bewildered. What just happened?

The look on his face is challenging, but there's a mischievous twinkle in his eyes. "My name is Jacques, Jacques DuPont." He puffs out his chest and straightens his spine. "My name is strong, *non*?"

"No."

He looks confused again. "*Non*?"

"I actually mean no, this time." I flash him a smile. "You do realise that 'Jacques' is the French version of Jack, or James? They're common names in Australia, so I'm pretty sure they'd be considered '*fade*,' too."

I'm trying to goad him, but he doesn't react. Only smirks. "I am not in *Australie*. In Paris, Jacques is a strong name."

"Okay, Jack." I grin at him, and this time his jaw clenches. Picking up the cup, lid, and tissue, I put them in a nearby bin, then remove a business card from my bag. "Call me when you've sent your suit to the dry cleaners." I hand the card to him. "Bye, Jack, and sorry again about the coffee."

I turn tail and dash off as I hear him call behind me, "It is Jacques!"

I chuckle to myself and rush down the road towards my office around the corner, realising with despair that I'm late for work and rather than having my usual coffee to sip on, I'm *wearing* it instead. Damn.

Minutes later, I reach the front door and realise I'm smiling. I don't remember the last time I turned up to work with a smile. I swipe my security pass, push on the door, and breeze into the open plan office with a cheery, "*Bonjour!*"

We have no receptionist since all customer contact is done online or over the phone.

The door clicks shut behind me as I remove my peacoat and hang it on the rack. It's early April, the second month of spring in Paris, but still chilly.

"Did you forget to wash your clothes over the weekend, Jane dear?" says a snobby, nasal voice to my right.

My smile slips, and I breathe in a slow, calming breath. The familiar shame and embarrassment threaten to overwhelm me, but I use all my strength to push it away. I broke up with my ex, Blake, for many reasons, but the main reasons were his controlling and untrusting nature.

Everything I did, everything I said, was wrong. Even what I *wore*. My clothes were either not fashionable enough or not the right style or colour. It was never *enough*. I'd hoped coming to Paris would let me finally be me...until I met Francine.

Slowly I turn to find her standing by the watercooler, her thin arm resting on top. With makeup applied too thick, dressed in a black miniskirt and a light blue blouse that shows off way too much cleavage, she tries hard to look twenty even though she's in her mid-fifties. Her blonde hair is so badly dyed it's tinged an icky yellow.

Although, I have to give it to her, her long legs are impressive for a fifty-odd-year-old, but she really should learn to dress her age.

"*Bonjour*, Francine," I say between clenched teeth. Every day I try to be civil and every day I wonder why I bother.

She raises her perfectly manicured eyebrows and views me critically from head to toe. Same thing every morning. Doesn't say anything else, just sticks her nose in the air and turns away.

This isn't a professional look, I understand that, but I don't go around in soiled clothes every day. I had no time to go home. So why is she always like this?

If I'm being completely honest, I think it's because of *who* I am. An average Australian girl who dresses for comfort, not fashion. I speak my mind when I need to but otherwise don't draw attention to myself. I'm easy-going and know how to have a laugh. But the kicker?

I learned quickly that Francine doesn't like change, so much so she's kept this company stuck in the past. If the décor is anything to go by, it hasn't moved past 1996. Then I, an outsider, am sent in and start making technology changes... It explains everything. Oh, and let's not forget the fact my boss, Claude, encouraged everyone to speak English around me. Francine hates speaking English; she told me so on my first day here.

I'm literally everything Francine *isn't.*

When Regina, my boss in Australia, posed this opportunity to me, I was so excited. Blake and I had just broken up, so getting away from him was ideal. I could go to Paris for six months. Implement a new database. Train the staff. Come home renewed.

Of course, life is never that simple.

Now I'm here, and Francine is the reason I'm so eager to go home. From the moment I arrived, she's made my life a living hell. It's all too close to home, being so similar to Blake and all.

I have tried to make friends, but my French sucks, which is issue number one. Issue number two is that when I do meet people who speak English, I have a knack for attracting the rude ones. The rest of my colleagues are friendly enough, but they're not social, and I don't enjoy Paris on my own.

My only two friends in Paris are Claude, my boss, and his wife Penny. She's Australian, too, and when we met, we had so much in common we became instant friends. We text daily, but we rarely see each other. We've met up twice in person, then she had a baby, and we couldn't see each other as often. Family comes first, I get that. I only wish I had someone to share Paris with.

Shaking the thoughts from my head, I dash to my desk in the hopes of making it safely without drawing more attention to my soiled clothes. Thankfully I don't have to train anyone today so I can hide in my nineties-style cubical and spend the day checking emails, filtering through tech support tickets, and troubleshooting any issues.

I bury myself in my work until fifteen minutes later when I'm disrupted by people whispering and pointing. Poking my head above the cubical wall, I spot Claude at the back of the office, just inside the doorway. He spots me and waves with a huge grin. I wave back at the same time I notice another man next to him. Since Claude is also tall, I can't see who it is.

Until the man steps forward and clears his throat.

It's Coffee Guy. AKA Jacques "Jack" DuPont.

Crap.

Chapter 2

Jacques

The office is still. Silent. A quick cursory glance around and I am not impressed. Claude warned me the office was a relic, but I did not expect it to be this outdated. Claude inherited the business recently after his *grand-père* passed away. Unfortunately, he was old school and liked to keep things the same. Now it is up to Claude to drag the company into the future.

Claude clears his throat and, in English, says, "I'd like to introduce Jacques DuPont."

Everyone turns their gazes to me, and I pull my shoulders back, head held high.

"I'm sure everyone will agree that clients are not attracted to a company that sells high-tech hardware but is still stuck in the past." Claude pauses and looks around.

I do the same, a few staff nodding in agreement. My gaze lands on a cubicle as a head of blond hair disappears behind it. I catch her face at the last second, and my eyes widen in surprise. It is the woman from the café. I frown as she lifts her head again and shrugs. Now that I think about it, she must be the Australian Claude told me about who is here implementing the new database. Yes, now it makes sense.

"The last six months' sales figures are proof," Claude continues. "Clients don't want an outdated website or office. That is why Jacques is here, to help lead Maître Tech into the modern world. Thanks to Jane's hard work over the last three months, we have new computers and a new database program, which is a great first step."

My gaze drifts back to the blonde. She is very pretty. Slim with long blond hair and large, round eyes. Blue, if I remember correctly. Pale skinned but with freckles on her nose and cheeks. Tall, too. I like that. The elitist French women I know would call her "plain," but I think she is beautiful. Unique.

"Jacques will assist the transition of Maître Tech by planning and overseeing renovations, staffing, advertising, and—"

"*Excusez-moi?*"

My attention is drawn to a shrill voice at the back of the office. To a middle-aged woman wearing young clothes. Her arms are folded, a look of thunder on her face. She is not impressed. Ah. This must be Francine, the one I am "assisting." Claude used a peculiar expression when he told me about her, one he learned from Penny. "Mutton dressed as lamb," he said. He laughed heartily, but I did not understand. Now I do. I bite the inside of my cheek so I do not laugh.

"*I* am the director here." Francine takes long strides into the office, stopping in front of me and Claude. "I am overseeing the changes and do not need assistance." She juts her chin out and looks at me like I am a pest. "*Monsieur* DuPont, you can turn around and walk back out of here."

I smirk at her. She thinks she is threatening. She is not. If anything, I find her pathetic. The idea of working with her is unappealing.

"Let us take this into your office, *Mademoiselle*," I say evenly. "Do not make a scene."

Francine huffs but strides back into her office.

"We will reconvene later," Claude tells the staff, and they all return to work. To me, he whispers in French, "I hope you're ready to face the wrath of Francine," then follows her.

I follow Claude and enter Francine's office, closing the door after myself.

"What is going on?" Francine demands in French, sitting in her chair. "I am capable of seeing the transition through to completion."

Claude sits opposite her, and I take the seat next to him. I relax now that I can speak in my natural language. I am completely to blame for my bad English. I learned it in school and am fluent enough, but I do not practice as much as I should. I never had any reason to until today. Claude's English is impeccable thanks to his years of travelling, then marrying an Australian woman. I have neither travelled nor married.

"Francine," Claude leans forward, "I have asked you countless times to provide me with estimates and plans, but I am yet to see them. You've been constantly working against the changes, especially Jane's implementation of the database. It's clear you do not want the transition to happen."

Francine shrugs one shoulder and inspects her nails.

I shuffle in my seat, glancing at Claude out of the corner of my eye. Claude filled me in on everything, and we agreed I would "assist" but be ready to take over if Francine proved difficult. I did not realise how difficult she might be. I am not happy that Francine is still performing in this role. After a few short minutes, I can see she is inept, and I am not convinced she will do it well.

I understand why Claude needs me.

Despite my reservations, I still need to give her every available opportunity, so I add, "I do not intend to take over. I only wish to help you."

Francine looks up, her gaze icy. "I do not need help." She turns to glare at Claude. "I told you I will provide what you need, Claude. If you give me another week, you will—"

Claude rubs his temples. "You've had three months, Francine. If you do not work with Jacques, he will have to take over your job."

Francine gasps. "No! What will I do?"

"You will join the others outside. Customer service, data entry—"

Another gasp and this time Francine lets loose a high-pitched squeal and slams her fists down on the desk like a petulant child. She glares at Claude, then at me, her eyes dark and angry, before swiping her arm across the desk, sending pens, paperwork, notebooks, and the keyboard and mouse flying onto the floor.

My anger spikes, and I send a fierce look to Claude, silently telling him this is inappropriate, and he should do something. If he does not, I will. He hesitates, uncertainty flashing across his features.

I open my mouth to say something when he speaks up. "All right, forget everything I just said." His face is red, nostrils flaring. "If you're going to act like a child, you're being demoted immediately, and I'm giving you a warning for inappropriate behaviour. You will pay for anything you broke out of your own pocket." Claude stands, the chair getting caught on the carpet and falling to the floor with a thud. "You will move out of this office immediately and into the vacant pod next to Jane."

Francine thumps the desk again, her eyes flashing with anger. I cannot believe what I am seeing. Why does Claude let her get away with it?

Claude leaves her office, and I follow as she squeals again.

Ignoring the staff who are staring at us, I follow Claude into his office and shut the door.

"You should have let her go," I say matter-of-factly. "She is not professional, and her behaviour is appalling."

"I agree, but haven't *you* ever lashed out when you've received bad news?"

I shake my head and frown. "No, I have not. There is never an excuse for that type of behaviour, Claude."

He sighs and sits on the corner of his desk. "Okay, you're right. Her behaviour *was* unacceptable, but I'm all about giving second chances, Jacques. I know your family would let someone go without a second chance, but it doesn't make it right. You need to remember *why* you left your family's company and started Solutions Exécutives."

Yes, I left because I did not like the unethical way my parents ran their company, Entreprises DuPont. Their treatment of staff and clients is disgusting. I have spent many years planning to bring Solutions Exécutives into fruition, and I want it to be a success. For that to happen, I must do things differently and be more ethical.

"I work on the three strikes and you're out rule," Claude continues. "I believe everyone deserves a chance to redeem themselves, even Francine."

I stare at my best friend for a long moment. We have been friends since we were boys even though we have had opposite upbringings. Mine was a privileged one; his was not. Despite this, he keeps me grounded and stops me going down the same path as my elitist family. He always teaches me a lot, and today his words stir something inside me.

I realise with a jolt that he is right.

My family does not care for its employees. One foot wrong and they are gone. No three-strike rule. I had never thought of it, but it is very fair.

"You are right, I apologise," I say with a nod. "But I believe there will be times when the rule will not apply if someone takes things too far."

"Yes, I agree," Claude crosses his feet at the ankles, "but I don't feel today's incident was that time."

I raise my eyebrows at Claude, not agreeing with him.

"Don't look at me like that." Claude looks away, embarrassed. "I'm not very good at this manager thing, but I'm working on it, okay? What's done is done. I've made my choice, and if it backfires, it's on my shoulders."

I say nothing else, not wanting to make Claude feel any worse. I understand how difficult this sort of situation is.

"I trust you know what you are doing," I say with a smile, so he knows I do not hold his decision against him. "I like your three-strike rule, and I will implement it in my business when I grow enough to hire more staff." It is just me right now, and Maître Tech is my first client, but I have a strong growth plan in place.

Claude grins and my chest lightens.

"Good man." Claude moves off his desk and slaps my shoulder. "Speaking of Solutions Exécutives, has your papa come to terms with you leaving?"

My jaw twitches as I grind my teeth and shake my head. "He is in denial and thinks I am taking a vacation this week. I must remind him I am not returning, but when I do, I suspect it will not go down well."

Claude squeezes my shoulder and smiles in sympathy. "You're doing the right thing. You know that, right?"

I nod, although a seed of worry starts to grow. I do not know what Papa's reaction will be, but I must be ready for anything because I am firm in my resolve to never go back to Entreprises DuPont.

"Good, now we should go and speak to Jane and fill her in before she gets a surprise visit from Francine."

Claude moves past me to the door and walks out.

I follow him, and we stop at Jane's desk. She is deep in her work, so she doesn't hear us. Claude clears his throat. She jumps and squeaks, spinning around on her chair. Her cheeks turn an adorable pink, and I smile. A warmth settles in my chest, and I get a fluttering sensation in my stomach. I like this woman, despite this morning's mishap.

"Oh, hi." She glances at me, and our gazes meet. Hold. I remember staring into her eyes at the café and seeing such genuine kindness, I could not help but like her.

She clears her throat, tucks her hair behind her ears, and turns to Claude.

"What happened to you?" Claude asks, slipping into English with ease. I am envious of how easily he can switch. I find it much harder.

There's no missing the coffee stain on Jane's blouse. I had time to go home and change, but she clearly did not.

"Oh, um," her cheeks grow redder, "a coffee mishap this morning."

I smirk but say nothing. I was annoyed when it first happened, but then I met this beautiful Australian woman who speaks terrible French, and suddenly I was not annoyed at all. She offered to pay for my dry cleaning, but I do not intend to follow through.

"Okay," Claude shrugs, "are you free at ten thirty? Jacques and I need to run a few things by you."

She checks the time on her computer and nods. At the same moment, another unladylike squeal comes from Francine's office followed by a string of French curses. Jane raises her eyebrows at me.

"Do not look at me." I raise my hands.

She turns to Claude instead.

He rolls his eyes. "I'll fill you in shortly. First, would you mind grabbing some coffees for us? I asked Jacques to, but he forgot." He elbows me in the ribs, and we grin at each other. I told him I forgot as it did not seem relevant at the time, not realising he knew Jane.

She removes a bag from her drawer and nods. "Only if I can have one, too, since I wore mine this morning."

She shoots a playful glare at me, and I cover my mouth to hide a smile.

"Of course," Claude says, "put it on the company credit card."

Claude turns and makes his way back to his office. I go to follow but then, having the urge to see Jane one last time, I turn back, only to catch her watching me. She flushes and turns away, but I do not miss the shine in her eyes. A look of interest. I see. That is how it is. I am not at all displeased. I, too, am interested.

A fluttering starts in my chest, and my breath catches. I grin and wink at her before turning and following Claude, enjoying a little too much that I caught her staring.

Jane

A shiver runs down my spine as I watch Jacques disappear. I should have learned my lesson when he caught me staring, but nope. I needed just one more ogle.

It's the dimples.

No, the wink.

Oh, I don't know. I already decided in the café that Jacques is handsome, but that wink and those dimples, they turn me into a puddle. Then on a different level, the way he handled Francine...wow. He was calm. Patient. Confident. Simply took her aside so as not to cause a scene. *Nothing* like Francine...or Blake.

Okay, sure, he was a little rude when we first met, but I *had* just spilled coffee on his suit. I remember the caution in his eyes earlier, and I sense there's more to this man. Enough to pique my interest. I swore off men after I broke up with Blake, never once considering I might meet someone in Paris.

Heat spreads through me, and my heart starts racing. My face is burning. I'm probably red as a freaking beetroot. I need air.

Grabbing my bag, I dash out, picking up my peacoat on the way out. Despite the sunshine, the air is chilly when I step outside. My burning face is thankful for this, but my body isn't, and I start shivering. I'll never adapt to the extreme cold here.

Donning my coat, I do it up to keep warm *and* hide the coffee stain. I only hope I don't wear *three* coffees this time as I can't afford to dry clean my coat *and* Jacques' suit. At least I'll be able to wash my own blouse. It isn't worth much.

The line is out the door when I arrive at the café, but it seems to be moving quickly. It's ten twenty-five a.m. by the time I grab the coffee and rush back to the office. I unbutton and shrug off my coat, hanging it up while managing to keep hold of the cup tray. I'm about to head straight to Claude's office when something catches my eye at my cubicle.

Or should I say, *someone.*

Francine.

At my desk.

I'm reminded of Blake once again and how he used to snoop through my things. Always so untrusting. I can't believe how similar those two are.

Gritting my teeth, I go over to her, but she doesn't hear me, so I stand waiting and watching. She's placed a pile of her belongings on the edge of my desk, and she's opening and closing my desk drawers. When she finds nothing, she stands up straight and huffs, placing her hands on her hips.

"Looking for something?" I ask.

Francine lets out a little shriek and spins around, wobbling on her too-high heels. Her hand flies to her chest. "Jane dear, you gave me a fright!"

"I said, are you looking for something?"

"No, nothing. I," she glances around like she's looking for an answer and, in the end, shrugs, "just realised I was in the wrong pod.

18

Silly me." She laughs, picks up her things, and dashes around to the empty pod next to me. After putting her things down, she disappears back into her office.

Wait. She's in a pod now? But she's gone back to her office. What the hell is going on?

I have a lot of questions.

"Jane!" Claude calls.

I hold up a finger to tell him I'll be a sec. I put my bag back in my drawer, but this time I search for the key and lock it. Since we've had no thefts before, I don't lock it, but after seeing Francine poking around, I don't trust her. What could she possibly want to steal from me? Either way, I'm protecting my things from now on.

I make my way to Claude's office and close the door after me, placing the coffees in the middle of the table. "Sorry I'm a few minutes late."

I grab a cup and take a seat, looking from Claude to Jacques. They're both wearing neutral expressions. Claude is always easy going, so when he's serious, it means something big is going down.

"What's going on?" I ask. "What's the deal with Francine's epic meltdown and the fact she's currently moving into a pod?"

Claude plays with a pen in front of him and looks at Jacques, who nods.

Claude thinks before diplomatically saying, "Francine doesn't have the company's best interest at heart."

I sip my coffee, glancing at Jacques over my cup. A couple of hours ago, he was just a random stranger I spilt coffee on. I wasn't too sure what to make of his appearance at Maître Tech, but after what I witnessed earlier, I'm impressed. He might even be trustworthy.

His eyes capture mine, and he gives a single nod as though confirming what I'm about to ask. "But Jack does?"

Jacques says nothing about the name I use, only smirks, but Claude looks confused. "It's *Jacques*," he pronounces it precisely and slowly, obviously thinking I just don't get it, "and yes, I believe he does."

"Even though he's never worked here before?"

Honestly, I have no idea where this is coming from. I'm only here to do a job, and I'm eager to go home, yet for some reason I'm strangely protective of this company. I arrived not long after Claude took over and have experienced a strong sense of satisfaction seeing some of the changes taking place. Francine aside, everyone else is hardworking, and they care about the company. I don't want it to go up in a puff of smoke.

Claude smiles softly. "I appreciate your concern, Jane, but you must trust me. Jacques and I have both spoken in detail and we're in agreement. I'm confident Jacques will move us forward." Claude sits forward, frowning. "I do have one favour to ask."

My skin prickles, and I have a feeling I know what he's going to ask. I nod for him to continue, but deep down, I hope I'm wrong.

"I need you to show Jacques the ropes around here. Introduce him to the new database and bring him up to speed on where we're heading."

I breathe a sigh of relief. I was wrong.

"*And*," Claude smiles mischievously, "keep an eye on Francine for me."

Bugger. I was *right*. Damn it.

"Claude!" I bury my face in my hands. "Don't get my hopes up, then dash them in the same breath!"

He laughs, and Jacques laughs, too. A pleasant sound, deep and velvety.

"Jack I can handle," now I mispronounce his name on purpose, "but Francine—"

"Don't worry about her," Claude says. "If she causes any issues, tell me." He looks to Jacques, then back at me, "Are you having trouble pronouncing his name?"

I stifle a laugh. Even Jacques smiles and shrugs in defeat. "It's a long story." I stand, coffee in hand. "I'd better get back to work. Good luck, *Jacques.*"

Claude nods appreciatively, but Jacques only stares intently at me, his face neutral. Did I murder the pronunciation of his name? That wouldn't surprise me. We say nothing more, and I leave the office.

It'll certainly be interesting working with Jacques. I *will* be professional around him, so long as he doesn't wink or grin at me too often, displaying those fabulous dimples.

On my way back to my cubicle, I spot Francine at the pod again, poking her head over her cubicle wall, looking at my things. What the hell is she looking for? I'm going to have to be on extra guard around her.

When she spots me, she smiles innocently and asks, "Jane dear, I need some help. I can't save my work."

With a deep breath and a prayer for strength, I go to her.

Chapter 3

Jane

F rancine is like a feral cat who's been let loose amongst the pigeons, with me and the rest of the staff as the proverbial pigeons. When she's not checking up on what everyone is doing, she's bugging me about one thing or another.

"Jane dear, why isn't this record saving?"

She's asked this *more than once*! The first time she couldn't find the save button, which is ludicrous as it's a blue button at the top of the screen. Impossible to miss. The second time it didn't save because she left some mandatory fields blank. How she missed this is also beyond me as the fields were outlined in red. The other three times she asked, I suspect she didn't press save because she wanted to annoy me. And she succeeded.

"My program crashed, Jane dear. Can you fix it for me?"

It hadn't crashed; she'd closed it down herself "by accident." Although it took me nearly an hour to come to this conclusion. *Ugh.*

"Oh no, Jane dear, come quickly! I think I deleted the shared drive! What do I do?"

She deleted a blank folder. A. Blank. Folder. Like seriously?

This has been going on for *two days*. I'm trying to give her the benefit of the doubt; after all, this must be difficult for her. But honestly, I'm at the end of my tether.

What the hell is it with this woman? My tolerance levels are at an all-time low. The next twelve-and-a-bit-weeks look very grim. And, another thing, what's with the "dear" thing every time she says my name? She's been doing it since I started, and it always feels so patronising. Is it so hard to say "Jane"?

Sighing, I glance at the time on my computer. Four ten p.m. Still fifty minutes to go. Francine is speaking to Jacques, probably to continue the handover they've been doing on and off over the last couple of days. I'm enjoying the peace for a short while.

Jacques' presence at Maître Tech has been great. He's *doing* something. He and Claude have been in and out of meetings, and there's finally movement on the modernisation project. An all-staff email was sent out yesterday with the project roadmap. The planned renovations for two months' time got everyone talking excitedly. Well, everyone except Francine, of course.

I haven't given Jacques a demo of the database yet; I'm supposed to be seeing him tomorrow. We don't speak often, but we always seem to run into each other. Literally. Going to or from the kitchen or bathroom. Leaving the café each morning since he arrives as I'm leaving. We've had no more accidents, but he's just *there*. Always.

And I can't get away from those damn dimples. Little smiles here and there, lingering glances. When I'm in his presence, I'm always left with burning cheeks and a racing heart.

Sneaking my mobile phone out of my desk drawer, I check for messages. While Claude is relaxed about us texting at work, he also doesn't like us to overdo it.

There's a message from Penny received a minute ago. I swipe to unlock the screen.

We've found a babysitter! To celebrate, Claude and I are taking you out for dinner.

Dinner sounds wonderful, but the truth is I can't afford it. Paris is so expensive, especially meals out. Getting paid every four weeks doesn't help, so it can be a real struggle. Since I'm used to getting paid fortnightly, it's been a big learning curve. I budget the important stuff, including my morning coffee, but I still find myself reaching the last week before payday with little left.

It's not something I want to admit, so I'm contemplating a diplomatic response when the phone vibrates in my hand. Another message from Penny.

You're not allowed to say no, either. Our shout. No arguments. We want to do this. Claude is organising the booking, so he'll tell you the time and place.

The opportunity to get out and experience Paris again, *with* people this time, is what makes me cave. I'll find a way to repay them somehow. I send a message saying thank you and I'll be there, then put my phone away and return to my work. With all support tickets actioned, I browse through my emails, seeing one from Regina. I go to click on it when an instant message pops up from Claude.

Got 5 mins? Need to talk to you.

My spine stiffens as I make my way to his office. Has Francine been in his ear and spreading stories about me already?

Great, now she's made me paranoid. Blake did the same thing, always had me doubting everything and everyone.

As I grab the door handle and turn, I tell myself it's nothing. Yet the butterflies still whip up a storm in my stomach.

I push the door open, and Claude looks up, his face serious. My stomach rolls as I close it, swallowing the lump in my throat. As soon as it clicks shut, Claude breaks out into a grin and relaxes back in his chair, resting his feet on the desk.

My shoulders slump as I plop into the seat with a sigh. "You scared the crap out of me, Claude."

"*Moi?*" He holds a hand against his chest and smiles innocently.

"Yes, you, and you know it. Looking all serious until I close the door. I thought I was in trouble."

Claude chuckles and places his hands behind his head. "Sorry, I couldn't resist. Besides, what would you be in trouble for?"

I shrug, unable to answer.

Claude lets it drop. "Did you get a message from Penny?"

"I did, and I appreciate the offer, but I'm paying you back somehow."

He shakes his head, his brown eyes bright and playful, reminding me of a big kid. In fact, that explains Claude to a tee. At work he's serious, but outside of work he's so much fun to be around.

"Not going to happen." He sits back and folds his arms over his broad chest, raising his eyebrows challengingly.

I lift my hands up in a shrug and let them fall to my lap. "All right, fine. It sounds nice, thank you. So, where are we going?"

"It's a restaurant on the river. Francette." Claude types something on his keyboard and presses enter. "I sent you the address." He sits back in his chair and puts his boss face on. "How are things going with Francine?"

I open my mouth to rant, but then I close it again. Instead, I say, "Nothing I can't handle."

Claude frowns. "You'd tell me if anything was wrong, though, right?" He lowers his face and captures my gaze.

I force a smile and nod. "Of course I would. It'll take a bit of getting used to, that's all. She's not used to being a regular joe like the rest of us out there."

As I speak the words, I realise how true they are. I mean, she's been demoted. That's gotta suck. I think *I'd* be hard to get on with if it were me. It's also the first time I have to work closely with her. I shouldn't throw in the towel so easily.

"You're not a regular joe, Jane." Claude's brow furrows. "You've helped this company take a huge step forward. Now with Jacques here, he'll take it to the next level." Claude leans forward and folds his arms in front of him on the desk. "Speaking of Jacques, I've been meaning to ask you, what's with the mispronunciation of his name? Your French isn't *that* bad."

I shrug and bite my lip, stifling a giggle. I can't *not* tell him about the incident. "Jacques didn't forget coffee that morning a couple of days ago."

Claude stares at me for a moment, head cocked to the side.

"I might've accidentally run into him at the café," I confess with an awkward laugh, "and we both wore my coffee. He must've had time to change, but I didn't." I explain how the Jacques and Jack thing came about.

Claude laughs and shakes his head, resting his right leg over his left knee. "You have no idea who he is, do you? Or who he's connected to?"

I shake my head. "How would I? I don't keep up with the Paris news."

"Maybe you should. The DuPont family has fingers in lots of pies around here. They buy up lots of businesses, modernise them, and sell them for a profit."

I sit upright in alarm. "Wait, they're buying this place?"

"No, Jacques is not here on their behalf. He's got his own business. He's here to help us modernise and move forward. The point is, he's a DuPont, and let's just say he's more privileged than the average person."

Breathing a sigh of relief, I settle back in the chair. "So you're saying he's not used to someone giving back as good as he gives?"

"That's precisely what I'm saying. Jacques and I have been mates since we were kids, I know what he can be like, so I'm glad you stood up to him. Don't get me wrong, he's not a bad guy at all, he's just a little blind to the goings on of 'normal' people."

I grin and sit taller in my chair. "Well, that's good, then. A stained blouse is worth it." I stand and check the time on my watch. Four twenty p.m. "I should get back to my desk. What time are we meeting tonight?"

"Six thirty, and wear something warm. It'll be chilly on the water."

As I leave Claude's office, I almost run into Jacques again. I smile awkwardly and manage to sidestep without clashing. Our arms brush lightly, and a violent shudder rips through my body right down to my toes. I glance back briefly, and he does the same. He grins, displaying those sexy dimples, and yep, the wink follows. Cue burning cheeks and racing heart.

I rush to my desk and sit down, burying my face in my hands. Why do I have to fancy him of all people? After leaving Blake, I never once considered jumping into another relationship. Until now. One chance encounter with a slightly cocky but sexy Frenchman is threatening to change my mind.

When my heart slows back to its normal rate and my cheeks aren't so hot, I open the email from Regina. She wants to organise a meeting to catch up on things. We've done this a couple of times so far, but the meetings are outside of my work hours due to the time difference. I hit reply and send back the best time and day that suits me.

I open another email, this one about a database update scheduled for the weekend, when I hear Francine's annoying voice.

"Jane dear, why can't I save—"

My tether snaps. I lasted two days, I think that's pretty darn impressive, but I'm done. *So* done. Is she actually serious right now? I spin on my chair and glare at her. "It's the blue button, Francine! The *blue button*. Is it that freaking hard? How many times have I shown you since Monday!"

Francine's mouth drops open, and she disappears behind the pod walls. I turn back to my desk and bury my face in my hands again. So much for cutting her some slack. *Ugh*. I shouldn't have snapped.

Drawing in a deep breath, I release it slowly, then stand. A few people are looking at me and smirking, nodding their approval at my outburst, but I feel guilty. Despite all the trouble Francine caused in the past, I don't then have the right to do the same thing. I'm better than that.

I wander over to her desk and clear my throat. My breath catches when I see the whites of her eyes are red with unshed tears. *Damn.*

"I'm sorry, Francine." I smile apologetically. "I didn't mean to snap. I understand how difficult things are for you."

She sniffles and grabs a tissue from her desk, dabbing her eyes. "*Merci*, Jane dear. I am not young anymore and am not very good at computers."

"It's okay." I point to the blue button. "That's the button there."

She clumsily moves the mouse to the button and clicks, but a heap of mandatory fields light up in red. She gasps in horror and holds her hands over her mouth. "What did I do? Did I break it?"

I run my hands down my face and hold back a groan. How can she be so computer illiterate? Surely, she had to use a computer when she was doing Jacques' job? Something's not right here.

Shaking my head, I breathe in deeply and once again show her how to save a record.

Chapter 4

Jane

I jump off the train and jostle along with the evening crowd. When I step into the evening air, I shiver. The tunnels are always so warm, bordering on hot, and it's always a shock to step into the cool air.

I pull my peacoat tighter around me and button it up, then open the maps app on my phone. I always thought I read maps well...until I arrived in Paris. Somehow trying to read everything in French takes map reading to a whole new level.

Too busy looking at the map and street names and locations, I take little notice of my surroundings. The Seine is easy to find, but the restaurant is another story. There are barges all along the riverfront. Private ones that are moored. Tour barges filling up with people for a night-time river cruise. Some are made into bars, restaurants, even retail stores.

I'm looking from barge to barge, looking for a sign that says Francette, but so far nothing. I check the time—six twenty-five p.m. The smell of delicious food makes my stomach grumble, and I hope this is a sign that I'm close. I spin around and walk backward, checking the barges I've passed just in case I missed it.

Nope. I spin around again and come face to back with someone. Unable to stop in time, I run into them with an *oomph*. Geez, it's a week for it! I gasp and stumble back, nearly losing my balance. The man I've run into turns, a look of irritation on his face.

Jacques.

Of course it is.

The irritation disappears and he grins, those dimples once again sending butterflies into a flurry in my stomach.

"Do you ever watch where you are going?" he asks with a wry smile.

"Why are you everywhere I want to be?" I counter.

His hearty laughter catches on the breeze and caresses me. The sound sends another shiver down my spine, and I realise I'm more attracted to him than I first thought. He intrigues me.

"You are cold?" He starts to remove his heavy coat.

"Oh no, I'm fine." I reach out and put my hand on his arm to stop him.

Stop him it does, but the unexpected touch makes his gaze clash with mine. I stop breathing for a few seconds as I drown in his chocolate eyes. The lights from the lampposts on the dock make the flecks of gold in them glimmer.

He's the first to avert his gaze, and I follow suit, clearing my throat. He shrugs his jacket back on.

"Uh, maybe you can help me, though." I look around, still unable to find the barge. "I'm looking for Francette, it's supposed to be a restaurant along the river."

Jacques raises his eyes heavenward. "*Oh là là*," he tuts with a shake of his head, "I say again, your French is very bad. You have not mastered the accent. You are very Australian. It is *Francette*." He emphasises it the accented way.

I shrug one shoulder, trying to show I don't care, but my cheeks are burning. For some weird reason, I want to impress him, and I feel chided. Then again, why should I? Why can't he accept me for who I am? Familiar frustration rises as I remember the countless times Blake did a similar thing. I don't think Jacques is like him, I'm getting different vibes, but these little things irk me.

Yeah, I like this guy, but I'm not taking his "better than everyone else" attitude. I'm going to take Claude's advice and stand up to him.

"All I did was ask for directions," I look him square in the eyes, "and you *still* insult how I speak? I'm proud to be Australian, and really, how can I be expected to have a perfect French accent when I wasn't even born here?"

His eyes widen as he stares at me, mouth agape. He appears genuinely contrite. "*Je suis désolé*, I did not intend to upset you."

Now that's *definitely* something Blake never did. Apologise. Jacques' apology in French washes away any remaining annoyance. I need to remind myself that he's not of my ilk, and I'm not of his. We can't always take offence at something said wrong or misunderstood.

And that's the major difference between Jacques and Blake. Jacques is from a completely different life and culture. Sure, I don't know him well yet, but I sense something different about him. Something raw and honest and open.

Blake was a bastard for no reason.

I release a breath. "No worries, Jack. I forgive you."

He narrows his eyes. "You like this name 'Jack,' do you not?"

"I sure do," I grin at him, "Jack."

Before Jacques can speak, I hear my name called. I spin around. Two arms are waving wildly a few metres away.

"Penny!" Forgetting Jacques, I run up to my friend. We embrace tightly.

We pull away and grin at each other. Their daughter, Amélie, was born two months ago, and we haven't seen each other since. Being a first-time parent must be tough, so of course I don't begrudge her, but I certainly do miss her. Texting and calling are fine, but not the same as seeing her in person.

"It's so good to see you!" Penny exclaims, embracing me again.

Claude joins us when we pull away and slings his arm across Penny's shoulders, kissing her temple. I smile at them, admiring how perfect they are together. They've both got brown hair, but where Penny's eyes are green, Claude's are light brown. He's tall, and she's much shorter, yet they just...*fit*.

"Hi, Jane," Claude greets with a grin. "You found it, then?"

I shrug. "Not yet. I'm still looking." I glance around, and sure enough, next to me on the right is a barge with "Francette" in lights in the window. "Oh, here it is." I smile sheepishly. "I was looking for it when I ran into—"

"*Bonsoir*, Penny, Claude," Jacques says beside me.

"Jacques, it's great to see you!" Penny comes up and kisses both his cheeks. "I'm so glad you could make it. I don't get to see either you or Jane much nowadays. Looking after Amélie is a full-time job."

I look from Claude to Jacques in surprise. Claude is too busy saying something to Penny, and Jacques just shrugs as though to say, "I didn't have a chance to tell you."

Claude turns to me when I poke his arm, brows furrowed. I lean in and whisper, "Why did you invite Jacques? Is this a setup?" I narrow my eyes at him.

I'm not too sure how to feel about this evening now. If I'm being honest, I don't mind, but I would've liked some warning.

"Does it matter if it is?" Claude grins, then squeezes my shoulder. "Penny talked me into it, and I couldn't *not* agree. You're both single, after all."

"But we work together. Isn't it unethical?"

"Well," Claude strokes his chin, "technically you don't. He's contracted, and so are you. Fair game, I say."

Penny grabs my free hand and drags me away. I glare at Claude, but he has turned back to talk to Jacques.

"You're going to pay for this," I hiss at Penny as she leads me to the entry. "You're a conniving little so-and-so."

Penny grins, her green eyes sparkling in the bright entry lights. "Claude told ya, huh? Hey, I'm a married woman, but I still have a stinking crush on Jacques. If I can't have him, the least I can do is get him hooked up with my bestie." She loops her arm through mine and squeezes. "Don't be annoyed, Jane. He's a good bloke, I promise."

"A bit arrogant, if you ask me."

"He just needs an Aussie girl to loosen him up."

I hum in response. Truth is, I can't be annoyed. If I were in Penny's shoes, I would've done the same thing.

Francette is a three-storey barge. The basement is a cellar, and the other two storeys are dining areas. We're seated outside on the second storey, which is level with the dock. The Eiffel Tower is stunning, lit up in gold. With a smile, I pick up my menu, and unsurprisingly everything is in French. I'm not going to embarrass myself by asking for their translations, but thankfully I understand enough to get by.

As though reading my thoughts, Jacques, who's sitting next to me, leans in and asks, "You understand the menu, *non*?"

I turn to him with a raised eyebrow. He's grinning at me. Rather than answering, I hold the leather folder up to my face so I can't see him. He chuckles and turns back to his own menu.

The waiter returns a moment later, and we all place our orders. The staff are friendly and the atmosphere is lovely. There are outdoor heaters all around, which takes the edge off the chilly breeze coming off the river. Accordion music is playing, giving us a real Parisian experience.

These are the types of evenings I wish I had more of. Yeah, I know I'm mostly to blame for getting myself into this lonely rut. I should've taken the initiative to get to know more people, instead of relying on Claude and Penny.

In any normal circumstance, I would have, but I guess the language barrier got the better of me. Rather than trying, I locked myself in my small apartment on weekends and watched Netflix. Perhaps meeting Jacques is a blessing in disguise.

And maybe we'll hit it off. I'm not one for long-distance relationships, but I've also never met someone like Jacques before. Anything is possible if you connect with someone. But what am I saying? I only met the guy two days ago, and I'm attracted to him. One day at a time and all that, right?

I look at Jacques, who's speaking animatedly to Claude in French. Penny, who's also fluent in the language, joins in occasionally. I would normally find it rude when people around me speak in a language I don't understand, but I *am* in a French-speaking country. I can only blame myself.

I like seeing Jacques so animated. Apart from the flirty winks and smiles, I've only ever seen his serious work side. In a more relaxed atmosphere, he's a different person. Not so uptight or cautious. I realise his professional image is all a front. He has a name to live up to; probably a certain behaviour would be expected. It must be hard.

"Like what you see?" Jacques turns to me.

I blink and look away, cheeks flaming. I didn't realise I was still staring and that he'd stopped talking.

He leans in closer, his shoulder brushing mine and his exotic aftershave wafting around me. "I am *trés heureux* you are here, Jane."

He's happy I'm here? Oh geez. I look back at him, our gazes connecting, and I swallow. "Me too," I whisper back.

"I meant what I said earlier," he continues. "I am sorry I upset you."

His apology in English this time seems to hold a different meaning. I didn't doubt he meant it last time, but this cements it in a way. Almost like he wants to be sure I believe him.

"I have a bad, what is the English word? Uh, *habitude?*"

"Habit," I offer.

"Ah, *oui,* that is it. I am afraid I have a bad habit of saying things I should not. Claude often picks on me."

"Picks on you?" I giggle. "Do you mean he 'picks you up' on it? As in he corrects you?"

"*Oui*, it is same thing, *non*?"

"Not really. Picking on someone is when you want to hurt them."

He looks confused for a moment. "Oh, *oui*, I understand. I mean in a good way. He is not mean."

I glance across at Claude and Penny, who are cuddled close together, talking and flirting like a new couple. You wouldn't know they have been together for three years.

"Claude wouldn't know how to be cruel," I say with a smile.

"*Oui*, he is kind. He is a good friend to me, even when I am not a nice person."

I frown at him. "I can't imagine you ever being a bad person, Jacques."

He smiles at me, his eyes lighting up. "You use my name correctly!"

I chuckle and shrug. "I'm sorry for that."

"*Non*, do not be sorry. I like when you call me Jack."

"You do?"

He gives a single nod. "No one else calls me that."

"Okay then...Jack." I grin at him, and he smiles back.

Under the table, he takes my hand and gives it a squeeze. My breath catches and sparks shoot up my arm and down to my toes.

"Jane, look." Jacques points out over the dock. "La Tour Eiffel."

I turn and gasp. The Eiffel Tower is sparkling!

Chapter 5

Jacques

Despite growing up in Paris, La Tour Eiffel never fails to take my breath away. Lit up in gold with thousands of flashing blue lights, it is a true spectacle. A strip of blue light at the top of the tower flashes on and spins slowly around.

It is so easy to ignore when it is in front of you every day. But with a view of it from my apartment, I can appreciate it daily. I do not take what I have under my nose for granted.

Tonight, it is more magical. Strangely, my heart is beating faster than normal. With Jane here, I feel things I do not understand. Every time she is close, I want to say and do everything right. I want to witness the beautiful smile that lights up her face and makes her blue eyes shine. I want her to see me for *me*. An individual. Not as *Jacques DuPont*, son of the mighty Marcel and Angélique Dupont.

We met two days ago, and even though we have not talked much, I can see she is someone special. And if Claude trusts her, I trust her, too.

Under the table, I am still holding her hand as she stares at La Tour Eiffel. It fits nicely in mine. It is so natural. I like it. Her skin is soft and smooth. With a jolt, I realise that I *like* her. I have not liked another woman for a long time. I am too busy for relationships, and my family expect me to date certain types of women. Only French ones, and from a certain class.

I do not want to abide by their stupid requirements. Jane would not meet their approval, but I do not care. I am an adult, and I can make my own decisions. Jane is the most real woman I have ever met.

Glancing at her, the lights of La Tour Eiffel flash across her face. Her eyes are wide, lips parted in awe, taking in the spectacular sight. The desire to kiss her comes out of nowhere, and I avert my gaze.

Squeezing her hand, I let it go, then reach for my wine, sipping it. I do not want to come on too strong. Two days is not long, and usually I do not move this fast. But Jane is making me do everything so differently. Even before when she chided me for correcting her, I was not angry. I was appreciative because I sometimes say the wrong thing when I do not fully understand the English language.

She is like Claude in that way, happy to tell me when I am slipping up. I like it a lot.

"Absolutely stunning." Jane's voice is thick with emotion.

In control now, I glance back at her. She turns to look at me, her eyes shimmering, and a shiver runs down my spine, *feeling* the same emotion she is. Overwhelmed. Enthralled. Enraptured. Someone else appreciating it as much as I do makes me happy.

The setup of Francette on the water gives the illusion that I could reach out and touch the tower. We are so close. While that is not possible, it is an easy walking distance of ten minutes.

"You have never seen La Tour Eiffel?" I ask, even though I know the answer. It is impossible to miss.

"Oh, many times! You can't live here without seeing it." She turns back to the flashing lights. "I've never seen it sparkling, though. I don't get out much." Her smile is sheepish when she returns her attention to me.

"You are *introverti*?"

She shrugs. "Sort of. I mean, I like my own company, but I also like going out. There's no one to share it with, and Paris is best experienced with other people."

"*Oui*," I nod knowingly, "I agree. Paris is *magique, non*?"

She smiles softly. "It really is *magique*."

I nudge my shoulder against hers. "You say that word well."

Her smile is brilliant, heart stopping. "*Merci*, Jack."

"That one not so well." I tut, but I wink so she knows I am teasing.

She jabs her elbow in my side, and we both laugh. I like how easy-going she is and that I can tease her. I find Australian people to be very likeable. They do not easily take offence. Penny is the same. I wish I was more like that.

Jane picks up her wine glass and takes a sip, the wine dampening her lips. Her tongue darts out to remove the moisture, and my heart flips. I draw in a sharp breath and take another sip of my own wine. I knew tonight was a setup, even if Claude did not say so. I agreed to come because I was intrigued by Jane, but I am thankful to Claude.

The waiter arrives with our food, ending further conversation. I do not go out with people often, so it is nice to be here. It occurs to me how lonely I am. I do not have many friends. Friends I can trust, that is. Most people who claim to be my friend only do so because of my connections and status. Claude is the only exception, but since the birth of Amélie, he and Penny have been preoccupied.

Maybe Jane will be someone else I can trust.

I glance at her. She's talking animatedly to Penny and Claude about her life in Australia. I enjoy hearing her stories. Her life is a far cry from my monotonous, boring, and lonely life here.

"Glenelg Beach was *the* place to be during summer," Penny is saying, her green eyes glinting.

Jane nods animatedly. "One of my aunties lives in Glenelg, so I used to spend every summer school holiday with her. When I got my licence and a job, I drove down every weekend."

Her life sounds so different to my own. What would it be like to have a life of freedom? One that is not always on display? One tiny slip and the whole of Paris knows. I cannot help being envious.

Penny's eyes gain a dreamy look as she pushes a piece of fish around her plate with a fork. "How did we never cross paths during the holidays? Can you imagine the fun we would've had?"

I glance between the two girls, confused. Did I miss something? How do they know each other? Jane's smile is sad, and I wonder what she is thinking.

"Claude and I are planning to visit at the end of the year," Penny exclaims, "so the family can meet Amélie. We *must* catch up."

Jane visibly perks up, sitting straighter in her chair. This must be good news. "Definitely!" She places her knife and fork diagonally across her plate. "They've got a pop-up bar that opens during summer on the beachfront. Live music, deck chairs, hot food, and plenty of alcohol."

Penny polishes off her fish and sighs. "That sounds amazing. I can't believe it wasn't around when I lived there."

"It's new-ish, but there's nothing better than sunset drinks on the beach..." She sighs and stares out over the dock and at La Tour Eiffel.

I have never experienced the sort of entertainment she talks about. It sounds enticing.

I sense a melancholy mood come over Jane. I hope she is okay. I shuffle in my seat, and she jolts as though breaking out of a trance.

"Have you ever visited Australia?" Jane cocks her head to the side questioningly.

A snort comes from Claude. "Jacques has never left Paris."

Jane regards me for confirmation, and I nod. "*Oui*, Paris is my home. There is no reason to leave."

Though as I speak those words, I question their truthfulness. I would like to leave. Travel. Experience the world. Despite the privileged life I grew up with, I have never been able to. Never encouraged to.

Perhaps I could visit Australia once Jane returns. An unexpected pang hits me in the middle of the chest at the thought of her returning home, to a country so far away. I must keep reminding myself that she does not live in Paris permanently. It is odd that I feel this so soon. Jane is certainly one of a kind.

"More like his family have him trapped here," Claude mutters, not bothering to keep his tone low.

I glare at him, but he shrugs, not seeming to care. Unfortunately, he is right, and I cannot be angry at him. I only wish he would not declare this to the world. I *am* trapped here because of my family. My only hope of leaving is my new business. If it takes off, I will have control of my life at last.

I told my parents about my new business venture, but they do not think I am serious. As I told Claude, they think I am only taking some time off working for them. I need to make them understand I will not be returning.

Jane's inquisitive gaze and the quirk of her eyebrow speak volumes. I smile at her but say nothing. Not tonight, at least.

When we're done with our meal, the waitress appears with a dessert menu and removes our plates. I am perusing it when Penny's phone rings. She talks into it, her eyes widening in alarm, then hangs up and picks up her bag.

"Amélie is sick," she says to Claude. She turns back to Jane and me, smiling in apology. "Sorry to cut our meal short, but we must go. We'll pay on the way out."

"No worries, you go, and thanks again for dinner." Jane stands and goes around to embrace Penny. "I hope she's okay."

Penny smiles. "I'm sure she will be. Stay in touch, yeah? We'll do this again soon."

Jane sits down as Claude and I shake hands, then he leaves with Penny.

"It is just you and me, *non*?" I turn to Jane.

Her cheeks are pink, and she does not meet my gaze. I realise this must be awkward for her. Claude did not say as much, but her surprise at seeing me earlier confirms she was unaware I was invited tonight. Now left alone when we barely know each other, I understand it might be uncomfortable.

To help her relax, I gesture to the menu. "Would you like dessert?"

She shakes her head. "No, thanks." She leans back in her chair and rests her hands on her stomach. "I'm full as a goog."

I blink a couple of times, trying to understand the words. English may be difficult for me, but this is a completely new word. I shake my head in confusion. "Goog?" I ask, the word unnatural on my tongue.

Jane's giggle confirms I said it incorrectly, but I love hearing her laugh, so I do not care.

"It is one of your Australian words?" I add.

"Yes, and may I just say," she clears her throat, and her Australian accent is more pronounced when she adds, "your Australian is very bad. You haven't mastered the accent, mate. You are very French. It's *goog*."

She is teasing me? I throw my head back and laugh. Hard. I do not laugh often, and it feels good. I am liking Jane more and more. Like Claude, she is no nonsense and carefree.

"*Touché*, Jane. I deserve that one."

She smiles smugly and sits straighter in her chair. "FYI, a 'goog' is an egg and the expression 'full as a goog' means being full."

I shake my head. "You Australians have odd expressions." I pause as I consider her last sentence, eyebrows drawing together. "What is FYI?"

"Sorry, Jack," she chuckles lightly, "I really need to stop using abbreviations. It means 'for your information.'"

"Oh, *oui*, I understand. Thank you for explaining to me." I pause, thinking of a way to spend more time with her, then ask, "Would you like ice cream instead? There is a place nearby."

Her cheeks turn pink, but I do not know why.

"That's still dessert," she retorts.

"Did your *mère* never tell you ice cream only slides down?"

She bursts out laughing. "I thought that was an Australian expression!"

Her laughter rings out around me. Some people look across and smile. It is literal music to my ears. I could listen to it all day.

"You have a beautiful laugh, Jane."

She stops short and stares at me. "I do?"

Has no one ever told her that before?

I nod, keeping our gazes connected. "Will you walk with me?"

Finally, she agrees to my idea and nods. "Sure, that sounds lovely."

We stand, she buttons her coat up, and we leave the barge together. I must thank Claude later for the meal. I offered to contribute, but he refused. Once on the dock, we walk in silence for a few minutes. Jane's eyes stray back to La Tour Eiffel, still lit up in all its magnificence but no longer sparkling. It will start again on the next hour.

When we cross a road, we get a perfect view of it from top to bottom.

"Wait," she grabs my arm to stop me, "let's enjoy the view."

Her touch does something to me, and all I want is to be close to her. She does not seem to mind when I position us so we are facing the tower and I slide my arm across her shoulders. It is nice. Natural. The faint scent of flowers from her beautiful blonde hair drifts up to my nose, and I lean forward just enough so I can enjoy it. My heart is racing again.

We stand like this for a long while. Not talking. Just admiring the beautiful landmark.

After a little while, we leave and walk in silence, my arm remaining around her shoulders. She stops suddenly, and I jerk to a stop next to her in surprise.

She points to a metro sign. "This is my stop if I want to go home tonight."

"Oh." I am disappointed. Jane is good company.

She seems to hesitate, so maybe I am not the only one. It has been a fun evening, and I enjoyed getting to know her. When she glances at her watch, I see the time, too. It is only eight forty-five p.m.

"You go to sleep early?" I ask.

"Nah, I'm a night owl. Shall we keep walking? I can get on at another station."

I smile and nod, holding out a hand to her. She takes it with little hesitation, a strange warmth spreading up my arm and through my body.

"Tell me more about your life in Australia," I say as we start walking. "Compared to your life now."

We step off the dock and onto a cobblestone path lined with French Baroque–style houses and buildings. Accordion music is coming from a nearby café, full to the brim with people needing their evening caffeine fix, the scent of coffee permeating the air.

"You want the truth?" she asks.

We step down off a curb and into a circular courtyard surrounded by old shops, all shut for the night, and a fountain in the middle. There are couples walking together, hand in hand, talking and taking in the sights. La Tour Eiffel is still visible, casting a golden light over the courtyard. We wander over to the fountain and sit on the edge.

"Of course," I say, letting go of her hand.

She clasps her hands together on her lap. "Honestly, not much different to here. The only difference is we all speak English." She smiles at me. "Otherwise, life is much the same. My social life has taken a hit, but I only have myself to blame."

"It must be difficult for you."

She shrugs. "Yes, but I should've worked on my French more so I could communicate better. When I found out I was coming here, I took some classes, but I didn't work hard enough. Then I arrive and the language barrier makes it difficult to meet people. Add to it that I find some people are…" She pauses as though considering what to say that will not cause offence. "…a little rude," she adds with an apologetic smile.

If only she knew, nothing she says will offend me. Her honesty and openness are refreshing.

"Ah, *oui*, I hear this often." I lean back and grip the edge of the fountain. "I confess we are a proud nation, and I am sorry you were made to feel unwelcome." An idea comes to me. "Perhaps I can show you more of Paris? Show you why we call it 'the city of love.'"

Her eyes widen, and I hear her breath catch. "I'd like that a lot."

"Tomorrow after work, we will have dinner."

"Are you asking me on a date?" She grins at me.

This is precisely what I am doing, but is it wrong? Have I overstepped a line? "This is a problem?"

She appears surprised at first, then laughs awkwardly. I realise she was not expecting the invitation. I suppose *I* did not expect it, either. It came out without me thinking, but I would definitely like to go on a date with her.

"No, not a problem." She rubs her nose and gives me a small grin. "Men don't ask me out often, especially hot Frenchmen."

"Hot Frenchmen?" I make a show of sitting straighter and puffing out my chest, making Jane laugh. "I do not believe you."

"That you're hot? Oh, but you are." Her grin turns mischievous as she rakes her gaze over me. When it reaches mine, her beautiful blue eyes are shining. Instinctively, we move closer. The desire to kiss her is overwhelming. Only an inch closer and I can press my lips against hers.

"I mean I cannot believe that you do not get asked out often." I take in her beautiful features. Her large blue eyes are spaced perfectly apart in her heart-shaped face, her full lips begging to be kissed.

"Believe it," she says with a sigh. "I'm considered a Plain Jane in Australia."

I shake my head. "A what?"

She chuckles and moves away, putting space between us. It is the safest move, but I miss her closeness.

"Plain Jane, it's an expression that describes a woman who is plain. Even more apt considering my name is Jane. A source of mockery my entire life, I tell you." She rolls her eyes. "I'm as far from the pretty blonde-hair-blue-eyed-girl stereotype as one can get. I've got pale skin that burns instead of tans, freckles on my nose and cheeks, I'm tall and gangly without a single curve, and fried eggs for boobs."

I sit back and grin at her. Yes, Jane is certainly one of a kind, and the more time I spend with her, the more I like her.

Her eyes widen, and she places her slender fingers on those ever-tempting lips and giggles. "I'm so sorry."

"*Non*, do not be, but I must disagree." I drink her in, head to toe, taking in every beautiful detail. "You are far from plain, *belle fille*. Everything about you is truly *parfaite*." Reaching out, I run my fingers through her soft, blonde locks. The strands slip through my fingers like silk, landing on her shoulders.

She breathes in sharply, and when our gazes meet again, her pupils are dilated. The temptation to kiss her returns with force. This time my hand cups her cheek, her skin soft but cool from the night air. Is it wrong to kiss so soon after meeting? I am struggling to resist Jane Collins.

A clock nearby strikes the hour followed by nine chimes, and I pull back. Perhaps this is the sign we need.

"Tomorrow?" I ask when the clock stops chiming. "Dinner?"

She appears to shake herself, as though breaking from trance. "Yes, I'd like that. It's a date."

I smile and stand, holding out my hand. "*Bien*. Now, I will take you home."

"You will, will you?" She takes my hand.

I nod. "Paris may be *magique*, but it is not always safe. I would not rest well if I let you go on the metro. We will walk back to my car, and I will drive you home."

She looks at me in admiration and squeezes my hand. "Thank you, Jack. I appreciate your concern."

I stop and turn to her. "You are *très spécial*, Jane. I want you to be safe."

I tug on her hand gently, and we start walking.

Chapter 6

Jane

A grin spreads across my face as I follow him with a skip in my step. *Special.* He thinks I'm special.

The smile stays on my face as we walk in silence to his car, my mind going over the wonderful evening. And, oh boy, what an evening it's been. One of the best of my life, I swear. My mum would say I'm wearing rose-coloured glasses, but I disagree. If anything, I'm probably being more guarded than usual. But I'm not hiding behind a wall, either. If a new romance is on the cards, I want to enjoy every moment.

The highlight was seeing the Eiffel Tower sparkling. It was truly spectacular. I can't believe I've never seen it in that state before. Still, being able to experience it with friends...with Jacques...*perfect.*

"Did you know Penny before you came to Paris?" Jacques asks from beside me.

I jerk out of my thoughts. "No, why do you ask?"

"You say something about it on the barge, *non*?" His brow creases.

I think back, trying to remember. "Oh! She lived in the suburb I often visited when I was in high school."

What a small world! Meeting a fellow South Australian in Paris? Not very likely. I grew up in the country and she was in the city, but we often frequented the same areas of Glenelg during the summer school holidays when I'd visit my aunty. How we never met is beyond me, but I wish we had. I like my friends, but I don't connect with them the way I do with Penny.

"We were saying how we wish we'd met all those years ago," I continue with a wistful sigh. "We could've become great friends."

"But you are friends now, *non*?"

I contemplate his words. "Yes, I suppose you're right." I know it's logical, but I was so focused on what we'd missed out on, I didn't consider what we had now. I'm *so* glad we met.

We continue walking in silence, and I sigh happily. It really has been a wonderful evening.

My cheeks warm when I remember Jacques suggesting ice cream. Oh, it was tempting, but my mind was running riot, imagining him eating ice cream, or more specifically *licking* ice cream, with those intense brown eyes on me... Oh boy, bad idea. No siree, ice cream is *off-limits*. Especially if I want to control myself and *not* throw myself at him. A walk was by far the safest option.

Even being close feels natural despite how short a time we've known each other. Holding hands under the table and while we looked at the Eiffel Tower after dinner. Him putting his arm across my shoulders. For a moment, I worried that maybe this was weird. I mean despite what Claude says, I still see Jacques as my colleague.

Yet strangely, everything feels right.

When you meet someone you connect with, you just gotta trust your gut.

To top off the night, Jacques DuPont asks me out on a date. Me! Plain Jane. Although I'm not plain to him. Jacques sees something I don't.

Jacques stops at a fancy black Peugeot with silver trim and presses a button on the fob to unlock the doors. He opens the door for me, and I give him a smile of thanks as I slide in. The new-car smell invades my senses, strong despite the pine air freshener hanging from the rear view mirror. Soft, leather seats. Glistening buttons and knobs. Good lord, this car is new. As in *new*, new.

Jacques gets in and puts his seatbelt on, asking me for my address. I give it to him, then sit stiffly in the seat, hands folded in my lap, too afraid to touch anything.

We're driving for a few moments when the seats grow warm. I could never afford a car like this. This man is *so* out of my league; why am I even letting him into my vastly different life? Not only that, but if I'm going home soon, I shouldn't get involved. It'll only end in heartbreak.

When he stops at traffic lights, he glances across at me and frowns. "I drive too fast for you?"

He appears genuinely concerned, and I smile to ease his worries. "No, your driving is fine." He's a good and safe driver. "I'm too scared to touch anything. Your car is so pristine and new. Nothing like my rust bucket at home."

My twenty-year-old Mazda has seen better days, but it still gets me from A to B, so I have no need to upgrade. Besides, I can't easily afford one without getting a loan. I've been debt free my whole life and don't intend to change that any time soon.

Blinking away my thoughts, I glance back at Jacques, who's staring at me in confusion. The light turns green, and I point to it. He turns back to the road and drives off. It occurs to me that I've done it again and used an expression he doesn't understand.

I chuckle lightly and pre-empt his question. "It's just an expression. My car in Australia is old and rundown. Not rusty as such, but still very old."

"You buy a new car, *non*?" He glances across at me briefly with raised eyebrows like it's the most logical thing in the world.

We're worlds apart, Jacques and me. And that's the other thing. How the hell would we even *work*? Our worlds are far too different.

I sigh and shrug. "I can't afford it."

He frowns, and we fall into silence. His brow remains creased as though he's in deep thought, so I stay silent. A slight unease settles around us. I hope I haven't offended him. If so, I don't know *how* since I was only telling him the truth.

Hold on. Why am I telling him *any* of this anyway? Earlier I didn't want to tell Claude or Penny that I couldn't afford dinner. Yet Jacques... I feel like I can be honest, and he won't judge me. I want him to see *all* of me. No surprises.

Jacques speeds through the streets of Paris as though he knows them like the back of his hand. I suppose he does if he's grown up here. One hand is on the steering wheel, deftly manoeuvring the car, the other arm resting on the door with the window down. The breeze catches his hair, but he doesn't seem to care, whereas it blows my long hair into my face. Each time I push it out of the way and behind my ears, it flies free within seconds.

Jacques turns a corner and slows to a crawl. A glance out the window tells me this is my street. Both sides are lined with identical Haussmann-style multi-storey apartment buildings, and the road is brick, not bitumen. I'm constantly in awe by how different the architecture is here compared to Australia. So beautiful and ancient. Australia's architectural history is so young in comparison. More modern and, dare I say it? Boring.

"Pull over here," I say, pointing. "My building is on the left, with the blue door."

He stops and puts the car in neutral. He turns slightly in his seat, and that intense gaze is on me again. I swallow and lose myself in it.

"I apologise for my ignorance, Jane. I am not familiar with your life and situation. I should not assume you have the same *liberté* I do. I hope I did not offend you."

That's what the uneasy feeling was between us? One thing going for Jacques is his ability to notice the difference between his life and others. He deserves credit for that, as few people can. Yep, including Blake.

Seriously, I need to stop with the comparisons. He's long gone; time to forget about him. For good.

"No, of course not," I say. "Our lives are different, that's all. You can probably buy a new car any day of the week. For me, my twenty-year-old car must tide me by."

Jacques' cheeks turn pink, and I curse my thoughtless words. He didn't choose this life; he was born into it.

"I'm sorry," I hastily add. "That wasn't an intentional dig at you."

His smile is tight, but his eyes aren't accusing or angry. "I did not take it that way." He reaches out and gently brushes his thumb across my cheek, his eyes taking in every inch of my face. "You are," his eyebrows draw together, "*une bouffe d'air frais.*" He looks at me eagerly, to see if I understand him.

His hand drops to his lap, and my skin is still on fire in the wake of his touch. My heart is racing as I interpret his words. I pick out the French ones I recognise until I piece it together. "Oh, a breath of fresh air, I understand."

He grins and nods. "*Oui.* You help me see beyond my privilege." His smile drops and he shakes his head. "People think I enjoy it, but I do not."

I want to know more, ask about his family. Delve more into Claude's passing comment over dinner. But a curtain has come down; his expression is blank. It's not a topic for tonight.

"I think it's great that you're willing to take the time to learn how the other half lives." I reach out and take his hand, linking our fingers. Heat surges up my arm and warms me from the inside out.

"I would like to learn more." He lifts our entwined fingers and kisses the back of my hand, his gaze capturing mine once more.

I can barely think. Or breathe. My head is spinning. Jacques is so distracting. I mentally shake my head and remove my hand from his so I can focus. The moment I do, I'm struck with an idea. "Tomorrow night, you're still showing me more of Paris?"

Jacques nods.

"Tell you what, you can be the tour guide and I'll bring the food."

He looks intrigued. "But we are having dinner together, *non*?"

"Of course, but it'll be dinner on a budget."

His face lights up, and he nods. "*Oui*, we do that."

Grinning, I reach for the door handle, then stop. I can't just leave without saying thank you or goodbye, but I'm suddenly tongue tied.

Turning back to Jacques, who's staring at me with a soft smile, I feel my insides go all jittery. I have this insane desire to kiss him, but obviously it's one hundred percent stupid. I mean, we only met two days ago. It would be completely inappropriate. Then there's the obvious fact that I'll be going home soon, and I definitely don't do flings.

I draw in a calming breath and smile at him. "I had fun tonight, thank you. And thank you for the lift home." I reach for the handle again and pull on it, the door swinging open, cool air rushing inside.

Jacques leans in, his eyes shining in the dull light of the car interior. For a split second, I think he's going to kiss me, and I know without a doubt that I won't pull back because it's increasingly clear I'm weak to all things Jacques.

Of course, he doesn't because he's a lot more mature and level-headed than me.

Instead, he moves his head to the right and kisses one cheek, lingering a few seconds longer than necessary. When he moves back, his gaze meets mine. Holds. Lips inches apart, warmth radiates off them before agonisingly slowly moving to the other side and kissing my other cheek. My head spins, eyes flutter close, and I breathe in his exotic scent.

I feel him move back, and I open my eyes again. His pupils are dilated, and his eyes flick to my lips momentarily before he pulls back further, putting distance between us. Smart man.

"*Bonne nuit*, Jane," he says.

My heart is racing, and I can't hide the tremble in my voice when I say, "Goodnight, Jack."

With a smile, I grab my bag and slip out of the car, walking to the door of my building. I unlock the door and glance back. Jacques is sitting in the car, waiting to make sure I get in safely. Smiling at him, warmth spreading through me at his thoughtfulness, I lift a hand in a wave, then go inside.

Jacques

I watch until Jane is out of sight, then sit back with a sigh.

Again, the urge to kiss her was strong. Too strong. I do not know what she is doing to me, but I am struggling to think of anything, or anyone, else. I learned so much about her in one night. Our lives are so different, but she makes me want to be a better person.

I know it was not intentional, but I felt chided when she reminded me of how far apart our worlds are. I bought my car only days ago. My old one was not even one year old. I got bored, so I bought a new one. No other reason. I realise now it was unnecessary and frivolous when I could have better used that money. I can thank Jane for teaching me an important lesson.

My family does not ever think of those in need, and sometimes I fall into the same trap. I am eager to do better in future and help those less fortunate than I am. I cannot change the life I came from, but I can learn to put my money to good use.

Putting the car in gear, I drive home. I am only five minutes away, so it does not take long. It is nine thirty p.m. when I walk inside my penthouse apartment. As the door closes behind me, I stop and take in my modern apartment with a sigh. Yet more extravagance. Expensive and modern, the epitome of the DuPont name.

I hate every fibre of it.

I enjoy the comforts with the best of everything, but there is no character. It is not homely. There is no personal touch. Even growing up in an expensive mansion never felt like home. What does home feel like, anyway?

My gaze drifts to the large TV hanging on the wall and the bare shelves around it. I enjoy reading and have many books in boxes. I will unpack them on the weekend and give the apartment some life.

While I own this penthouse, I did not choose it myself. My parents chose it for me because it was expected of the DuPonts. They did the same for my brother and sister.

From now on, I will take control of my life and my business. This has been a long time coming, and I am determined to make Solutions Exécutives work.

Claude's business is my first client, and I am confident it will lead to other bigger clients. I am aware that Solutions Exécutives will be a competitor to my parents' company, but that was always the point.

At Entreprises DuPont, my parents pay a large sum of money to buy out a sinking company, modernise it, and build it into a successful one. The client is led to believe they will enter a fair partnership with Entreprises DuPont. My parents step in and follow through with the promise of turning it into a success, then sell it for triple what they paid the client initially. Sometimes more.

Due to cleverly worded legal documents, the client does not see the profits they should be entitled to. While it is legal, in my opinion it is an unfair and dishonest practise.

Solutions Exécutives will be all about transparency. I wish to provide my clients with a choice. They can hire me for a set fee to come in and modernise, but they will continue running the business once I am done. Or they can choose to sell after the modernisation, but I will be open and honest about the sale price and the percentage they will receive at the end.

Kicking my shoes off and leaving them in the entryway, I remove my phone from my pocket and ring Papa. The time has come to clear up any confusion and remind him that I will not return next week.

"*Bonsoir*, Jacques," Papa answers. "*Tu appelles tard.*"

"Hello, Papa, sorry to call late. Did I wake you?" I sit on a stool at the kitchen centre island.

"*Pourquoi parlez-vous anglaise?*" He is asking why I am speaking English.

"I wish to improve my English, Papa. You should do the same."

He huffs. "*Je ne parle pas la langue inférieure.*" He refuses to speak the inferior language.

I sigh, but I do not push him. "Okay, Papa, but I am going to keep speaking English, and I know you can understand me." He grunts but does not speak, so I continue. "I started my new contract today with Maître Tech."

Silence.

"That is not one of our clients," he finally says in English.

I sigh and sit on the sofa. "No, Papa, it is *my* client. Under my new business. I told you last week, remember? I am not working for you anymore."

Silence again.

"You are a competitor to Entreprises DuPont?"

I swallow. "Yes."

"You are a traitor!"

"How? I am allowed to make my own life choices. I choose to start my own business."

"You disrespect the DuPont name! If you continue down this path, you will be cut from my *héritage*. You will no longer be welcome in this family."

The threat cuts deep, and I turn cold. I did not intend to cause a rift, but if I must, then so be it. Our family is not like others. There has never been any love or warmth, always run like a business. I am not close to Maman, Papa, or my siblings Rémy and Céleste. I am not sad or indifferent. I feel...nothing. A result of years of bottled-up emotions, I suspect.

The most unnerving thing is the idea of not having the money I grew up with. Still, money is not everything, and I must prepare for the reality.

"You will have nothing but your meagre trust fund," Papa adds.

He means to be threatening, but he is not. I laugh despite myself.

"Meagre? My trust fund may be smaller compared to the family money, but I am prepared to live off it if I must. It is enough to keep me going for a long while."

Unlike my family, who spends because they can, I try to be frugal and make smart investment choices to set me up for a better future.

The purchase of my new car recently was an accidental oversight. The point is, my money is mine, and they have no control over it anymore.

Despite my determination, there is no stopping the shiver running down my spine. I cannot deny that losing everything is an unsettling thought.

It might be the right choice, but it is not an easy one. It may take a while to come to terms with this, but I must. I cannot go back on my word and let Claude down. I need to prove I can do this.

Papa harrumphs. "You will regret this, Jacques. I am giving you three weeks to change your mind. After that, you are on your own."

Chapter 7

Å

Jane

The next morning, I wake up smiling. *Smiling*!

Geez. One good night with a handsome Frenchman and an innocent kiss on the cheek—okay, *two*—and I'm an emotional wreck. The last time I woke up smiling like this, I was twelve years old and had just experienced my first kiss the night before. In hindsight, it was a pretty terrible kiss, but that's not the point.

The point is, I'm a lost cause. A kiss on the cheek isn't even a proper kiss.

Kicking the covers back and sitting up, I notice my small apartment as though for the first time. My *appartement d'une chambre* is my little home away from home.

It's so small, the kitchen, dining room, lounge, and bedroom are all open plan, and the bathroom is separate, albeit small. But it does have a bath. The apartment is old, as evidenced by the dated kitchen cupboards and stovetop, along with the ancient plumbing in the bathroom. It has a modern black-and-white theme, with more use of white. It's affordable, too, considering its location in Le Marais.

I swing my legs over the side of the bed, and my feet touch cool tiles. I shiver and reach for my robe on the armchair next to the bed, donning it.

I walk over to a double window and open the two panes. It's not a balcony as such, but there's a concrete ledge with an iron railing.

I tighten my robe around me and take a step closer to glance out the window. The cool, spring breeze kisses my skin, and I breathe in the Parisian air scented with the flowers from the small planters on my neighbour's ledge. When the wind grows stronger, I catch the delicious scent of bread and croissants.

My stomach growls, reminding me I need to get a move on. That's the other upside of where I live: I'm close to work, the café, and the metro. Getting around is easy as pie. I close and lock the windows, then rush to get ready, eating a quick bowl of cereal as I do so.

Fifteen minutes later, my hair is blown dry and I'm dressed a little more sophisticated in black slacks, a turquoise cashmere jumper, and black flats. According to Mum, who bought me the jumper before I left for Paris, the turquoise makes my blue eyes shine. When I'm done, I check myself out in the full-length mirror and remind myself that I'm *not* doing this for Jacques.

I'm not.

I laugh at my own expression and shake my head. I'm a terrible liar. My heart skips as I turn away, remembering the innocent cheek kisses last night. I unplug my phone charging on the bedside cupboard; the time on the screen reads eight a.m. Half an hour to grab a coffee and go to work.

With my handbag over my shoulder, I leave my apartment and skip down the five flights of stairs and onto the street. Somehow, everything looks different today. Last night did wonders, and not just because I was with Jacques. More because I was reminded of what I'm not seeing every time I walk out my front door. I miss so much because I keep my head down and go from A to B so I can get through this torturous experience as fast as possible.

But it's not torturous...not really. Paris is so beautiful. There is so much to see, so much to do, and I need to embrace it. So today when I step outside, I take everything in. The Haussmann architecture, the accordion music filtering through the alleys from nearby shops, voices of people saying *bonjour* as they open for business or on their way to work.

As I walk to the café, I wave good morning to the locals and greet them with a bright smile. People are a lot more pleasant when *you* make the effort first. It occurs to me that my own bitterness would've surrounded me like an aura, and I wouldn't have been very approachable.

Gosh, a lot can change in such a short time.

My happy mood doesn't shift when I enter the café and place my usual cappuccino order. Even my French is better today! Although this could be a figment of my imagination. Whatever the case, everything is just *better.*

The normal work dread is missing, too. Francine? Pfft, I can deal with her. She's just out of her depth. I need to stop comparing her to Blake and stop being so paranoid. I should help her adjust. I know I haven't made *her* working life very easy. Especially after my little episode yesterday.

Everyone else might've appreciated my outburst, but it was unprofessional. Claude didn't say anything, so I assume he didn't hear about it, but it can't happen again. Today, things will be better.

When the barista calls my name, I pick up the coffee. I make my way to the door, stepping back when it opens as patrons enter. A lady holds the door open for me, and I smile a thank-you before ducking out onto the pavement, thankful to have no run-ins with Jacques, or anyone else for that matter.

It's going to be a good day.

⁂

The morning goes off without a hitch. Francine hasn't asked a single question, and we're both civil to each other. It's like my little spat yesterday, as unprofessional as it was, made a difference. I'm cautiously optimistic that we're turning a corner. Perhaps we *can* work together.

Although it hasn't even been a whole day of this new Francine. Only four hours have passed, so I better not get ahead of myself. When lunch time comes around, I contemplate asking her to join me, but when I glance back and find her scowling at something on her computer screen, I change my mind. Baby steps and all that.

Usually, I'd pack lunch and sit on a bench outside to eat if the weather is pleasant. Today I'm doing well on my budget and the sun is shining, so I decide to go to the café where I get my coffee from instead. They've set up outdoor tables and chairs and umbrellas to ward off the afternoon sun. This makes me chuckle because to me the sun holds no warmth and I'm still wearing my peacoat. The wind chill is still so high, the umbrellas are unnecessary. That's the Australian in me, I suppose.

As I approach the café, I see it for what feels like the first time. Hell, it probably is. I'd never noticed the wooden sign hanging from the verandah with "Café de Paris" in cursive writing. I've always called it "the café." I also never noticed the ivy climbing the side walls or the hanging flowerpots outside the entrance.

The cobblestone streets are lined with rectangular cement flower planters, flowers in bloom, trees, and other people on their lunch breaks.

Before going inside, I breathe in the scent of coffee and bread, mixed with the nearby flowers. Smiling, I turn to go inside and join the queue.

After placing my order, I find a table outside, lower the umbrella, then take a seat and enjoy some people watching. I don't normally do this, but after last night I need to take in everything. I don't want to miss anything else.

The streets are narrow with multi-storey buildings on both sides. The sunshine has brought everyone out. The sidewalks are lined with people chatting as they walk to their destinations. As I watch, I realise that despite the foreign country I'm in, people are generally the same.

The middle-aged woman dressed in the latest fashion walking her dog, who trots obediently beside her. The group of teenagers with their heads down, looking at their phones. The groups of coworkers chatting, coffees in hand as they return to work. The joggers or walkers who take advantage of their lunch breaks for exercise.

Yet despite the similarities, it's still so different somehow. It's oddly disconcerting.

My food and coffee arrive, and I thank the waitress.

"*Voulez-vous que le parapluie soit levé?*" She points to the umbrella.

I don't understand much, but I recognise that *parapluie* is umbrella, so I assume she's asking if I want her to raise it. I shake my head. "*Non, merci.*"

The waitress looks at me like I'm weird for enjoying the sunshine, shrugs, and walks away.

Thoughts of Jacques makes me smile. I relish in the memories of last night as I enjoy my lunch in the sunshine. For the first time, I'm at peace in Paris. Today is the first day I haven't checked how long it is until I go home. In fact, I don't want to think about it at all. I want to enjoy the time I have left.

I polish off my panini, take out my phone, and make a list of items to buy after work for my date with Jacques. A picnic is my plan. The most budget friendly option I can think of. A fissure of excitement skirts along my skin.

When my hour is up, I make my way back to the office with a skip in my step. Let's see if I can end the day well. If Francine continues to be civil, it just might. I'm also meeting with Jacques to show him how to use the database this afternoon. Time in his company *and* time away from Francine? Bring it on!

With a grin, I open the door to the office. Removing my coat, I hang it on the rack when Claude calls out to me. I turn to find him half inside his office and half outside.

"Got five minutes before you see Jacques?" he asks.

I nod and Claude grins before disappearing. I haven't been able to ask how Amélie is yet, but the fact he's here is a promising sign.

Before going to his office, I turn and glance out over the pods when I spot Francine actively snooping in my drawers. She opens the top one, moves things around, then closes it. Repeats for the second one. What the actual hell?

I want to stop comparing her to Blake, but how can I when she's practically the female version of him? The critical looks and comments, the constant snooping and untrusting nature. It's why I have no control over my next actions. Too many memories, too much anger. It all rises to the surface, and I act without thinking.

Storming up to her, I grab her arm and yank her away. "What the hell, Francine?"

She stumbles back on her too-high heels, swaying slightly and rubbing her arm, her overly made-up face contorting in shock. There's a momentary stab of guilt in my gut, but I'm too angry to care.

"*Excusez-moi*? What do you think you are doing?" She adjusts her white blouse with a huff and tugs on the hem of her mini skirt. Why she bothers I have no idea; it won't get any longer by tugging on it.

"Why are you going through my drawers?" I place my hands on my hips.

"I am looking for a pen." She sniffs and flicks her hair over her shoulder.

"And you were looking for a pen yesterday, too, I expect?"

Uncertainty flickers across her features, but it disappears quickly, and she pulls her shoulders back, nodding. "Of course. Why else would I go through your disgusting drawers?" She sniffs again as though my drawers have come from the sewer.

They haven't. Just saying. They're your typical office drawers, and I don't keep food in them.

"You could've *asked* me." I glare at her. "Is that so hard?"

"Jane," Claude calls, a hard edge to his voice. "My office. *Now.*"

I don't realise I'm yelling until I witness Claude's unimpressed scowl. I lose all my puff and my shoulders slump. I *had* to ruin the day by losing my cool. Again. When will I ever learn? Francine brings out the worst in me.

No amount of telling myself to give Francine a chance is sinking in. I'm too suspicious of her. Perhaps I shouldn't be, but looking for a pen? Come on, everyone knows where the stationary cupboard is, next to the printer. Besides, I've got multiple pens in my top drawer, which she overlooked.

Francine smirks and prances back to her pod like she owns the place. I don't dare look at anyone. As it is, I can sense their eyes on me. I especially avoid looking at Jacques' office. I can't bear to witness disapproval. Or worse yet, pity.

I put my bag in the bottom drawer, triple checking I lock it, then glance once at Francine before making my way to Claude's office. I tuck my drawer key into my trouser pocket for safe keeping. It was only unlocked because I went to lunch, and since I had my handbag with me, I figured it would be okay. Clearly not. If I can't trust her when nothing personal is in there, how the hell can I trust her when my belongings *are* in there? My cash, ID cards, *company credit card.*

Reaching Claude's office, I go in and close the door, plopping on the seat opposite him. We stare each other down, and my frustration diminishes. Arms folded, his usual bright and jovial light brown eyes are raging with anger and frustration. I've never seen him annoyed, let alone at me, and I hate that I made this happen.

We have a great working relationship and an even better friendship. He doesn't need me making our work life difficult. He accepted me no questions asked, was the one person who helped me settle in, and repaying him like this is wrong.

"I thought I told you to come to me if you were having problems with Francine," Claude says evenly, but I can tell he's only just holding it together.

I rub my lips together and think about how best to answer without annoying him further. "She was going through my drawers," I say, hoping the absolute truth will be enough.

As I say the words aloud, I realise how petty it sounds.

Claude uncrosses his arms and sighs. "Is that all?"

He's right, yet my automatic reaction is to defend myself. "What do you mean, is that all? I keep my personal things in there."

He pinches the bridge of his nose and releases a slow breath, slumping in his chair. He doesn't seem so angry now, but I know I'm treading on thin ice. "I heard her say she was looking for a pen. Is that such a problem? And besides you were at lunch and had your belongings with you."

"That's not the point, Claude. I caught her snooping around them yesterday while my belongings were inside. I don't trust her."

Petty or not, I *will* stand by this.

Claude sits forward and looks me square in the eyes. "I understand your concerns, Jane, but there are more mature ways of dealing with it. Disturbing the entire office isn't how you solve a problem."

Conceding, I sigh and sit back in my chair, letting my arms fall to my sides. "I know, I know, and I'm sorry. She's got this uncanny way of pushing that one button that gets me from zero to a hundred within seconds."

Claude smiles softly now, and I breathe a sigh of relief. We're still okay.

"Please try and control yourself, Jane. It's not a good look to the other staff or the company." His smile drops, and he shuffles in his seat. "As it is I have to officially give you a warning."

I cover my burning face with my hands, groaning into them. I'm mortified! I've never been given a warning for anything. Ever. If I want to see my contract out, I need to pull myself together and stop letting Francine annoy me.

"I promise I'll try harder." I smile apologetically.

"I did hear about yesterday's little episode, too. Don't worry." He gives me a stern look. "But I'm letting that one slide because the last couple of days have been difficult for both of you. I can't from now on, you know that."

I nod and give myself a stern talking-to. I'm an adult, after all. "I understand, Claude. Thank you." I go to stand but stop. "What did you want to see me for in the first place? You called me in when I got back from lunch."

"Oh, yes." Claude grabs his mouse and clicks on his screen a few times. "I've forwarded you an email with the next training schedule. Apparently, there's an important update coming to the program?"

I nod, remembering the email I received yesterday. "You need me to update everyone on the changes?"

"Yes, thank you."

I nod, then stand and step to the side. "How's Amélie?"

Claude looks confused. "Fine, why do you—" He snaps his mouth shut and his cheeks turn pink. "Oh."

A smile stretches across my face, and I shake my head, chuckling. "You and Penny are the absolute worst! Using your own daughter to set me and Jacques up? Seriously!"

I don't know the facts, but I'm assuming Penny must've secretly texted someone to phone her. She's going to pay! Although I *did* enjoy my time with Jacques, so I guess I should thank her.

Claude grins. "Hey, it was Penny's idea, and quite frankly, it was worth it. Did you enjoy the rest of your evening?"

My face feels hot again, and Claude's grin grows wider. Damn my pale skin!

"Then the night was a success," Claude says matter-of-factly. "All I ask is that the two of you behave yourselves on company time."

My skin grows hotter, and Claude laughs. Muttering under my breath, I turn and leave the office, his laughter ringing out after me.

Chapter 8

Jane

J acques' office is small. Too small. We're both sitting on the same
side of his desk so I can demonstrate the database. There's little
space between us. The door is closed to give us privacy, but I'm
tempted to open it again. It's hot in here, and the temperature is
rising.

Don't get me wrong, I'm not complaining. Each time his leg
brushes against mine, or his arm presses against me, I get a shiver
from head to toe. But I need to focus. On *work*. I should not be
thinking about kissing him. Nope, definitely not thinking about that.
Last night I concluded it would be one hundred percent stupid to
kiss him, and I'm sticking to it.

"What is this?" Jacques leans forward to point at the screen. As he
does so, he leans across me, and our arms press together. I breathe in
his cologne. Not overpowering, but fresh and woodsy with a hint of
pine. It's been playing havoc on my senses for the past two hours.
Each time I breathe in, my mouth waters and my head spins. He
smells divine.

He sits back again, and I fumble my way through answering his question. And fumble I do. His closeness and his scent make it next to impossible to answer something I should know like the back of my hand. I'm acting like I've only had one day of training, not months.

Would it really be so bad to kiss him? Was I too rash last night? A little flirting and harmless kissing won't hurt anyone, right? I'm a free woman, a *thirty*-year-old woman, who wants to settle down. Why not have some fun in the meantime?

Pull it together, girl.

Shaking my head, I pull my shoulders back and continue showing Jacques the database. He catches on easily, which doesn't surprise me, and listens intently. He's got so much restraint. Doesn't once flirt or get distracted. *He's* got it together. I should learn from him.

Besides, when at work, I need to be professional. Claude's orders.

When we're done, I breathe a sigh of relief and turn to him. "Any other questions?"

Jacques shakes his head. "You teach well, *merci.* Your program is intuitive."

"I'm glad you think so. The focus was simplifying the processes of entering and retrieving data, so my team in Australia will be glad to hear this."

I sigh, suddenly feeling homesick. Last night and even this morning, I was so much more positive. That I *could* survive the next three months. I had so much fun last night, but now I realise it was only one night. I still miss my life, family, and friends *so* much.

Jacques gaze is questioning. "You miss being home, *non*?"

How does he read my thoughts so well? I force a smile and nod. "I do, yes. I miss everyone, but mostly I think I miss the ease of life.

I don't have to think about what I'm doing. Here, I'm so out of my depth. In Australia, people are easy-going. When foreigners come to visit, we're all, 'Hey, mate, come over for a barbie and a cold one.' I come here and everyone gives me a wide berth like I stink."

Jacques cocks his head to the side. "You say barbie? It is a *poupée*, *non*?" His brow creases as he shakes his head in disbelief. "Your life is *very* different."

I stare at him agape. *Poupée*? What the hell is he—

"Oh!" I burst out laughing when I translate *poupée* to mean doll. "No, not *that* sort of barbie! Barbie as in short for 'barbeque.'"

All confusion vanishes from Jacques' face, and he laughs, too. Such a deep, velvety sound it sends a flutter to my heart and goose bumps along my skin.

"Your Australian expressions are peculiar," he says with a chuckle. "But you do not smell bad."

He leans in closer and inhales. If it were anyone else, I'd find it weird, but he's not being weird at all. If anything, I find it extremely *sensual*. A shiver runs down my spine when he nudges my hair with his nose. My resolve of not kissing him flies out the window. If he turns his head a little, I could lean in and press my lips against his.

He pulls back a little, his face only inches away from mine. "*Tu sens trés bon*," then adds in English, "like flowers and sunshine."

Oh my. Hearing Jacques tell me that I smell very good is my undoing, and I swear any second now I'm going to be a puddle of goo on the floor. That's got to be a better alternative than kissing while on the clock.

But I can't move. My heart is beating so fast and so loud, I can't hear myself think. There are bells going off in my head, telling me

I'm at work and this is a terrible idea, but nothing is popping this bubble any time soon.

So much for Jacques being more restrained than me. I underestimated him.

He closes the gap, his lips brushing mine in barely a whisper, making me whimper. All resolve gone, I'm ready to make out with Jacques right here, right now, when there's a loud knock on the door.

We jump apart. My heart is racing. Hands trembling. Sheer force alone has me turning back to the screen quickly, pretending to show Jacques something, while he calmly settles back in his chair, resting his right leg over his left knee.

The door bursts open, and Claude pokes his head in with a grin. I'm certain we appear natural, but his eyes narrow as he looks between us. Maybe he suspects something? Or maybe he's checking up on us to make sure we're behaving.

Nothing to see here, Claude. Nothing at all.

He says nothing, and my heart rate slows.

"Jacques, can I borrow you when you're done here?" Claude asks.

I smile and stand on trembling legs. "We've just finished, unless Jack has any more questions?"

His eyes glint when he smiles and shakes his head. "*Merci*, Jane."

I slip behind him and out of the office, closing the door after me. I stop outside for a few seconds, drawing in a couple of deep breaths to calm down. That was way too close. We need to rein it in. During office hours at least. Tonight is another story.

Giddy excitement skirts along my skin as I make my way back to my desk, no one paying me any attention. They have *no* clue what transpired in that office. My face heats up, and I sit down with a sigh.

As I come back down to earth from my emotional high, doubt tries to creep in along with logic. Is this wise? If I want to settle down, shouldn't my focus be on finding Mr. Right?

Jacques and I live in different countries and there's no way in hell I'm going to live here. From what little I know of Jacques, I'm certain he won't come to Australia, either. So, you see, it's over before it even starts. Wouldn't it be best to stop before anyone gets hurt?

Stop. Thinking. Have some fun for once.

Shaking my head, I push all thoughts aside and remove my desk drawer key from my trouser pocket. After checking everything is in my handbag in case Francine turned into Houdini while I was away, I close it again, happy that nothing is out of place. I glance behind me, just making out Francine's head. She hasn't even looked at me, let alone spoken, so hopefully that means the rest of the day will go off without a hitch.

<hr>

At five p.m., I leave work, and on the way home I grab what I need for our date. Once home, I dig out a picnic basket I bought on a whim the first month I was here. I had all these plans involving a picnic by the Seine, but it never eventuated.

Until now. Not that I know if we'll end up by the Seine, that's for Jacques to decide. He's the tour guide.

By the time everything is packed, with a baguette sticking out the side for effect and covered by a red-and-white checked cloth, I'm ready for our date. Dressed in jeans and the same jumper from work, deciding it *does* enhance my eyes as mum said, and Doc Martens, I feel pretty enough, but will I be warm?

My intercom buzzes at six thirty p.m. as I reach for my peacoat. Better to be safe than sorry. On the intercom display screen, I see Jacques at the door, looking around. I press the button to talk. "I'm on my way down."

I pull on my coat, then grab my things, tucking my purse and keys inside the basket. I dash down the five flights of stairs to the ground floor, pushing on the exit door and rush outside, nearly running into Jacques. He steps back in time, and I stumble to a stop with a giggle. I'm giddily excited.

Our near-kiss kept me excited yet nervous for what the evening might bring. I *am* going to have fun tonight. Live a little. Not overthink anything.

"Hi!" I push my hair back from my face with my free hand.

Jacques smiles at me, then looks at the basket with a raised eyebrow. "That is very French."

I grin at him and rest the handle of the basket in the crook of my arm. "I need to impress you somehow."

He turns serious and shakes his head. "You do not need to impress anyone, *belle fille*." He reaches out and strokes my cheek, his beautiful eyes roaming my face. "Being you is all you need to be."

My heart flips, and when he leans in swiftly, brushing his lips against mine in a chaste, sweet kiss, it leaves me wanting more. He pulls away quickly, and I groan. His grin is smug as he slides his arm across my shoulders and leads me to his car. My legs are like jelly, my lips are tingling, and I'm wearing the silliest grin on my face.

We reach Jacques' car, and after placing the basket on the backseat, I slide into the front. When Jacques gets in, there's no stopping me. I lean over, grabbing his face in my hands, and kiss him. Properly.

His strong arms wrap around me as he returns it with fervour. His lips are soft, his breath warm and minty, his scent of clean, fresh pine invading my senses.

Pressed against his chest, my heart races in time with his. Sparks fly between us to every nerve ending, awakening desires. His tongue begs for entry, and I grant it, our kiss growing heated and passionate. He's an experienced kisser, no doubt about it, and my head is spinning. I want to stay like this forever.

We pull away a few moments later, breathing heavily. The windows have steamed up, and I'm working up a sweat in my coat. Not that I care. *Totally* worth it.

Jacques gazes into my eyes and whispers, "*Vous êtes si belle*," before placing a lingering kiss on my cheek, then turning back to the steering wheel.

Hearing him tell me I'm beautiful makes my racing heart swell with *something* for this man. Only a few days ago, he was a stranger. We spend a few hours together, connect in a way I have never connected with any man before, and feelings are developing. *Strong* feelings. Too early to label them, but they're certainly growing.

He starts the car and moves forward. I settle into my seat and pull my own seatbelt around me.

"Okay, so you're the tour guide, remember? Do you know a good picnic spot?" I ask as Jacques turns onto the main road.

"Ah, *oui*, dinner on a budget, you say?" He inclines his head to the basket on the backseat.

I nod. "Yep. I hope you don't have any food intolerances?"

He stops at a red light, his brow furrowed. "What is this word 'intolerance'?"

"Oh, uh, is there anything you can't eat? Foods you might be allergic to or that you don't like?"

"Oh, I understand. *Non*, I eat too much." He pats his impressively flat stomach and grins at me. "My *famille* often says I will get fat if I keep eating."

"All families say that," I say with a chuckle. "But you've got nothing to worry about. You look great."

The light turns green, and he speeds off. "We go to Île de la Cité, a good area for eating *en plein air*."

Chapter 9

Jacques

It is seven p.m. when we arrive at Île de la Cite, one of my favourite places in Paris. An island in the middle of the Seine, it is away from the hustle and bustle of the central city. I take Jane to the eastern point where there is a grassy area with a pair of triangular flower beds. The early-evening springtime sun is lowering in the sky, bathing the area in a golden glow. Grey clouds are gathering up on the horizon, promising rain overnight and possibly tomorrow.

April has been unseasonably cold so far. Some days I expect snow, but it never happens. We had no snow during winter, which is unusual. It is not normal to have winter without it.

Clasping Jane's hand in mine, I lead her toward some benches overlooking the grass. Memories of when I was a boy come to me. I had a French au pair who would take me here sometimes when Maman and Papa were working. She would teach me all about the history of Paris then she would let me play to my heart's content.

They were the rare happy moments in my childhood. Her name was Aimée, and she was not just an au pair but my friend. Rather than treating me like a pesky in-the-way child like my parents did, she saw me as a growing boy who wanted to learn, play, and have fun. And she let me do all those things.

Until one day she got sick.

I knew she was sick, but she acted like it was not a problem. I am not sure what happened to her. When she never returned, I wondered what had happened. Did she get better? Did she die? My life after that was never the same. Maman took over raising me, and I could no longer be the boy Aimée allowed me to be.

My eyes sting with moisture, and I swallow to cover the sudden emotion. I have not thought about Aimée for a long time. Shaking the thoughts from my head, I force myself back into the moment. With Jane. A woman who is much like Aimée, I realise. She is kind, caring, and does not judge me for who I am.

I stop on a cement path surrounding the grassy area, lined with trees, lampposts, and wooden benches. "This is the heart of Paris," I announce proudly, holding my arms out wide.

The Seine is visible either side of the island, and beyond on both sides are rows and rows of historic buildings. A small stone wall blocks out most of the breeze coming off the water. Being away from the busiest parts of Paris, it is quiet. Even the birds can be heard as they settle down for the night.

"This is where Paris was founded." I turn and point over to some trees. "Over there is Cathédrale Notre-Dame."

Jane looks, holding her hand above her eyes to block out the sun. I hear her breath catch, and when she looks at me, her eyes are wide with awe, shining in the sun.

"This is amazing, Jack." She leans in to kiss my cheek. "Thank you. Let's eat. This is a perfect spot." She squeezes my hand, then walks off with the basket, stepping over onto the grass where large shadows from the buildings and trees behind us stretch across it.

I hold a hand to my cheek, scorched from her kiss. If I am not careful, I could easily fall for Jane. Our situations are so different, I do not know how we will work. Not just the money, that does not bother me. But the distance. It is clear she has no plans to stay, and I have no plans to leave.

Yet I do not want to be apart from her. I want to explore what we might have. Now that we have kissed, I never want it to end. Jane is remarkable; that is the only English word I understand well enough that explains her.

Locating a bench, I sit and wait for Jane, thinking she is looking around. But then I see her laying the cloth from the basket over the grass in the last patch of sun. What *is* she doing?

She glances back at me and grins, waving me across. "Come on!" she calls.

I stare at her in surprise. She wants us to eat...*on the ground?* With a shake of my head, I go over to her.

"There is a perfectly suitable bench over there." I point back to the bench.

She kicks her boots off and settles down on the cloth, grinning up at me. "I know, but it's not the same as having a picnic on the grass. Now take off your shoes and sit down." She pats the space next to her.

Before I can even think, my reaction is instinctive. "Do you think I, the son of Marcel DuPont, would sit on the grass?" I say with a sniff. "I am not removing my shoes and—"

Her unimpressed look says everything, and I realise how like my father I am. Even repeating the words Maman used to tell me—"You are the son of Marcel DuPont." *Mon Dieu.* I am not supposed to be that person anymore. I do not demand liberties or expect to be treated differently. The rest of my family does, but not me. Not anymore. Well, I try. Sometimes I slip, because it has been hardwired into me. I am always learning.

"Don't be such a snob, Jacques," Jane says. "If you don't want to take off your shoes, fine, but sitting on the ground isn't beneath you."

She avoids my gaze as she drags the basket across and starts unpacking the picnic food. Her words are curt but not malicious.

I cannot take my eyes off her. I am chided yet halfway in love with her just by a few truthful words. Because she is not afraid to stand up to me and tell me when I am wrong, just like Claude does. But unlike Claude, Jane is a sensual woman who I am growing more and more fond of every day.

I only wish she would call me Jack all the time.

While she unpacks, I sit beside Jane and untie my shoelaces. Slipping my shoes off, I place them neatly next to me, but I leave my socks on. It is too cold to remove them. As I do so, I am reminded once again of Aimée. Of doing a similar thing—having a picnic on the grass after my history lesson. It was summer, so I took off my socks, too, and ran around barefoot on the grass, loving the way it tickled the soles of my feet.

I am a far cry from that boy, but it is not too late to introduce some of that carefree time into my current lonely life.

"Isn't that better?" Jane asks, interrupting my thoughts.

I look across at her as she grins, wiggling her toes in her thick socks. I smile at her and shrug. "*Je suis désolé.* I did not mean to offend you. I appreciate that you, uh, pick on me the way Claude does." I frown, knowing I did not say it right again.

Jane laughs and nudges my shoulder with hers. "It's 'pick me up,' Jack. I'm not picking on you."

"Ah, *oui,* I get it wrong again." I chuckle and shake my head. It is an odd expression, one I struggle to use correctly. Claude uses it when he is, how does he say it? When he "picks me up on something I have done wrong." That is it!

Wrapping my arm around Jane's shoulders, I pull her into my side and kiss her temple, needing to show her I appreciate her honesty.

"And you didn't offend me." Jane discards the basket to the side. "I'm sorry if I was too...forward."

"*Non,*" I move away but take her hand, linking our fingers together, "do not apologise, Jane. I do not like being the arrogant and entitled person my parents made me." I pause, then add in a soft voice, "Please keep calling me Jack. I feel like you are angry at me when you call me Jacques."

She laughs. "I've got you hooked now, haven't I?"

I nod and think about why I like it. "I like it because no one else calls me Jack. It feels like you see me for *me.*"

Her eyes widen, and she looks at me as though peering into my soul.

Kissing the top of her hand, I hold her gaze and add, "When I am Jacques, I feel like that entitled and arrogant person I do not want to be anymore. You see beyond that to the person I want to be. *Merci.*"

"You're welcome," she whispers, reaching out to stroke my cheek. I lean into it, her touch sending sparks to my toes. "I do see you, Jack. I see a thoughtful, caring person who wants to do good."

Warmth starts in my chest and spreads through my body. If only she knew how much those words bring me pleasure.

"Let's eat." She grins and turns to the food.

My stomach growls in appreciation when I admire the spread before us. A baguette, butter, French mustard, pâté, pickles, camembert and gruyere cheeses, smoked ham and chorizo, grapes and strawberries, and finally a bottle of champagne.

"You create a good *charcuterie*," I say.

"Thanks, I hope you're hungry."

"*Affamé.*" I reach for the baguette and rip the end off.

"Oh, here." She reaches into the basket and pulls out two plastic champagne flutes, serviettes, and some plastic cutlery.

I eye the plastic with instinctive distaste, but this time I catch myself before I can react. Pushing past instinct, I quite like the ease and affordability of them. The packaging has "*biodégradable*" splashed across it, too, so I appreciate that they protect the environment.

We spend the next hour eating and talking. It is a truly wonderful evening. I do not remember the last time I sat and talked to anyone. Jane regales me with more tales of her life in Australia, and I listen intently, soaking up the vastly different life she leads. A loving family. Close friends. An easy-going life with no one to answer to. It all sounds so unreal.

I tell her a little about myself, that I own an apartment, and I have a brother and sister, but there is not much else to say. I might have had a privileged upbringing, but not an interesting one. I do not say much else about my family because I do not like talking about them or their questionable business practices.

They are not nice people, and I hope she never meets them. They will be unjustly mean to her because she is not of their class. I do not want to put her in that situation.

Of course, Jane is an inquisitive woman, and it does not take long for her to ask questions. "What do your mum and dad do for a living?"

I pick a grape off the bunch and eat it as I contemplate how to answer. I stare ahead at the dark sky, the soft breeze coming off the water ruffling my hair. The sun disappeared behind buildings a while ago, and we are now bathed in dull, unnatural yellow light from the nearby lampposts.

"What did Claude tell you?" This is the safest option as I know he would not say anything bad.

"Not a lot," she answers, finishing off her second flute of champagne. She pours herself half a flute more and holds the bottle out to me, but I shake my head. If I am driving, one is my limit. I see the approval in her eyes and know I have pleased her.

"Just that your family owns a company that buys out other companies," she adds as she puts the half-empty bottle back in the basket. "Something about modernising and selling them at a profit?"

I stare out over the river where a barge full of tourists is floating under a bridge. "That is it, but their business is not always *honnête*."

"Honest?"

I nod. "So I leave the company and start my own. I modernise and help them grow. If they decide to sell, I will be fair in giving them their share of the profits."

She is staring at me, but what is she thinking?

"Claude is my first contract," I continue, tugging at blades of grass beside me. "My family is not happy with my decision. My papa threatened to remove me from the family *héritage*." I sigh and grind my teeth at the memory.

"Is the inheritance really that important?" Jane places a hand on my arm and squeezes lightly. "You've got your own money to live off, don't you?"

I nod and turn to her, my stomach rolling uncomfortably at my possible future. Yes, it is a risk I am willing to take, but it is not an easy one. To take a step into a world I have never been exposed to before is overwhelming.

"But you are right," I give her a bright smile in the hopes she does not see how I am feeling, "it is not important. I must do this." I nod once in confirmation. "I am independent, *non*? I do not need their money."

Jane smiles and squeezes my arm again. "No, you don't. You're talented and business savvy, and you're going to go a long way. You'll make your own money honestly, and by what you've told me, that's what counts, right? I think it's really brave what you're doing."

Her approval touches me deeply, and I turn to capture her gaze, smiling softly at her. I am so fortunate to have met such an amazing woman.

"*Merci*, Jane. You are very kind." Then I lean in to kiss her.

Discussion closed, we fall back onto the soft grass, the cool breeze washing over us. Our kiss is slow and lazy. Jane's flowery scent mingles with the sweet grassy smell, and she tastes of champagne and cheese. We stay like this for a long while, until time has no meaning and for a few blissful moments, my worries are nothing but a passing memory.

Chapter 10

A

Jane

I close my apartment door after me and lean against it with a long sigh, my eyes fluttering close.

What. A. Night.

Good lord, I'm in *deep* trouble.

As if being on the literal island where Paris was first founded wasn't awesome enough, being with Jacques made everything *perfect*.

When his snobbish trait slipped through with the whole sitting-on-the-grass thing, he was quick to apologise. I saw it on his face, the moment he realised what he'd done. And *I* learned something, too...that Jacques isn't choosing to be snobby or churlish. It's hardwired, and sometimes he slips up. I respect the move he's making to stand on his own two feet. It must be tough walking away from family. Can he do it? Only he can decide that.

Then learning more about him, about his plans away from the family business and wanting to make a difference, he's a man I can truly fall for. One who cares about others and wants to put his money and his skills to good use.

Yet despite the fact his father threatened to remove him from the will, and Jacques probably only has a trust fund to live off, which won't last forever, he's still insistent on making a difference.

With another sigh, I open my eyes and push away from the door. After brushing my teeth and changing into my nighty, I crawl into bed. Turning the light off, I snuggle under the covers when I realise with a sinking sensation that if I'm not careful I might fall for him.

Then I'll want him to be my Mr. Right when he's entirely Mr. Wrong.

Groaning, I pull the covers up over my head and will sleep to take me away, to a place where it's just Jacques and me. Forever.

***

I sit at the little two-seater table in my apartment and open my laptop. My eyes are drooping as I open Zoom. I log into my meeting room and admit Regina, my boss from Australia, moments later. Her smiley, grainy face pops up next to mine.

Her long, red hair is piled on top of her head and a colourful scarf is wrapped around it. Large, gold hooped earrings hang from her ears, and her makeup is somehow bright yet subtle at the same time. The colours suit her complexion and draw focus to her best features—her green eyes and plump lips. Regina's got this way of pulling off the overdressed look. She wears oversized, colourful clothes with tons of jewellery and manages to look stunning in the process.

"Hi, Regina," I greet, stifling a yawn.

It's Sunday night, and I've had a lazy day today, but I'm exhausted. Why are lazy days often more tiring than busy ones? I'd usually be in bed by now for a full eight hours of sleep before work, but Regina insisted on our meeting being nine a.m. her time, which turns out to be eleven thirty p.m. here.

"Jane, hi!" Regina's shrill voice comes through my crackling laptop speakers. "You look *amazing*! Have you done something to your hair? Are you using a new skincare product? You're practically *glowing*."

My cheeks flush. Today Jacques was busy so I didn't see him, otherwise we've seen each other every night since our last date on Thursday. Geez, that man can kiss. We haven't gone further than heated make-out sessions, but holy moly, it won't be long before I drag him back here.

One day of not seeing him is enough to cause major withdrawals. Tomorrow can't come quick enough. Maybe I'll even ask him back here afterward.

Who knew being ravished daily made someone glow? You learn something new every day.

"None of the above," I say. "In fact, I'm dead on my feet. I should look like a zombie."

I smile when Regina's laughter tinkles through the speakers. She's a good boss, and we've always had a great relationship. She's one of the people I miss most. She's older than me by fifteen years, but we've become close friends. Outside of work, she's my closest friend and confidant.

"Well, either way, Paris seems to be agreeing with you," she says. "And I'm getting nothing but positive reports from Claude." She leans in closer to the camera and in a lower voice asks, "Is he single by any chance? We chatted on Zoom for the first time the other day, and oh my God, he is to *die* for." She fans herself. "You know I'm a bit of a cougar. I like 'em young. What is he? Thirty-ish?"

I laugh. "About that." I can't be sure, to be honest, but I assume we're a similar age. "And I'm sorry to break it to you, Reg, but he's married with a baby."

Regina sighs. "Damn. Oh, well, guess I'll to stick to the limited Aussie blokes around here. Talk about man drought." She rolls her eyes. "Have you met a hot Frenchman, Jane? Is *that* why you're glowing?"

Bugger. I'd hoped not to bring Jacques into it, but I'm also terrible at lying. I can't say no as she'll see it on my face straight away. The best I can do is downplay it, so she doesn't overreact.

"Okay, I might've met someone, but it's nothing special. We've been on a couple of dates, nothing serious."

Regina's eyes grow wider. "Jane! Oh my God, tell me more!"

Shuffling in my seat, I bring the conversation around to my work performance. "Reg, there's nothing to tell. And anyway, I thought this was supposed to be a work call? Not to be rude, but I'm shattered and would like to sleep sooner rather than later."

This is true, but I also don't want her making a big deal about our relationship. There is too much stacked against us. Not only the fact that we're from different worlds, but neither of us wants to move countries. Who knows? Maybe we'll figure something out. Maybe we won't. A lot can happen in the nearly three months we have together. But this is exactly why I don't want anyone to know.

Regina smiles sheepishly. "You're right, and I'm sorry. I forgot about that." She straightens in her seat, and a shutter comes down over her face. Boss-mode enabled. "So, I have good news and bad news. How do you want it?"

My stomach drops. "Good news first." Most people would choose bad news first, but I'm not like most people.

Regina gives a single nod. "They love the work you're doing. They love the database and appreciate the time you've spent implementing it and training them."

I grin, breathing a sigh of relief. Even though Claude tells me I'm doing well, I like hearing it from another person. Sometimes people embellish feedback when they tell you face to face, but they won't hold back in saying what they *really* think when feeding back to someone else.

Before I let it boost my ego too much, I reluctantly ask, "What's the bad news?"

Regina looks at her desk rather than the camera. "You'll see a contract amendment in your inbox when you log in tomorrow morning. I'm afraid they don't have the funds to keep you on for the whole six months. You'll be coming home at the end of May now, instead of July."

I stare at the screen, mouth agape. She wasn't joking when she said it was bad news. My mind is racing, a thousand questions cramming for space in my brain. Regina looks up, her brow creased in worry. This must've been bugging her the whole weekend. How did I not know anything about this? Why didn't Claude say anything?

He *had* been suspiciously quiet on Friday. Barely even spoke to me. I assumed he was busy. Now I know there was more to it, and he was avoiding me. Well, I'll be having words with him tomorrow.

Is it weird that I'm hurt by this? Yeah, I'm only a contractor, but up to this point, Claude and I have been honest with each other. Why not this time? Why so secretive?

"End of May?" I squeak, my voice not sounding like my own. I do a quick calculation in my head and slump in my chair. "But...but that's only six weeks away."

"Jane, I'm *so* sorry."

She continues talking, but I don't hear her, too busy going over the contract in my head. Was there anything about allowing amendments after it had been signed? I'm a stickler for this sort of thing, and I read it back to front dozens of times. Then I recall one clause in the fine print. Something I shrugged off thinking it wouldn't be relevant. About the sponsor being able to amend the contract in extreme circumstances.

Ugh.

"Jane?" Regina calls, concern lacing her voice. "Jane? Are you okay?"

"Sorry." I rub my forehead. Placing my elbows on the table, I rest my head in my hands and release a long, slow breath. "It's ironic," I lift my head with a weak smile, "a week ago, I was so eager to come home. Now—" I shake my head and squeeze my eyes shut, holding back tears.

Now, Jacques has imprinted himself on my heart and the idea of leaving him makes me sick to the stomach. This sucks! Nearly three months cut back to six weeks. Does this mean we're doomed?

Why does this hurt more than it should? I was never meant to grow attached to Paris, or anyone *in* Paris for that matter. And this is exactly why.

"Why didn't Claude tell me?" I cry, a traitorous tear sliding down my cheek. I wipe it away quickly.

"Don't blame him. I was the one who told him I'd contact you before you went back to work on Monday. I didn't want you to find out by reading your emails."

"Oh." I chide myself for overreacting. "Of course, I appreciate it. I'm shocked, that's all."

"At least it's nothing personal. If we can find another company in Paris to use our program before the end of May, I'll be able to utilise you. But so far nothing, I'm afraid. As a last resort, you could find a new sponsor, which would mean a new job, but I shouldn't say that too loudly. I don't want to lose you."

Pulling myself together, I force a smile and shake my head. "Reg, it's fine. These things happen. That's why we have a contract, right?"

The timing is so off. I *knew* getting involved with Jacques was a bad idea.

Yeah, a new job *is* an option, but I enjoy where I work. Now everything is complicated. That said, I wouldn't change a thing. If it ends up being a fling, so be it. If it doesn't...well, who knows?

"We're still marketing for new clients." Regina's clearly trying to add a positive spin on it. "Perhaps the company you're working for can spread the word, too."

I nod mechanically, keeping my forced smile in place. "Of course, I'll tell Claude. Thanks, Reg."

"Are you okay?" She leans forward so her face is close to the camera.

"I'm fine, Reg. Is there anything else I should know? Otherwise, as much as I hate cutting our conversation short, I need some sleep."

Regina slowly shakes her head. "No, that's all. Next time we'll swap our meeting times, so I have to meet you at an ungodly hour."

"Sounds good. Say hi to everyone in the office for me. I miss you all."

We end the call, and I realise it's true. I do miss them. Like all workplaces, there are one or two people I don't necessarily get on with, but overall, we're one big family. Despite how much of a blow Regina's news is, a part of me is looking forward to seeing them again.

Closing my laptop, I rub my tired eyes and get ready for bed. It's well after midnight when I slide between the soft sheets a few minutes later.

How am I going to tell Jacques the news? How will he react? I reach across for my phone to text him, then stop. We exchanged numbers before the weekend, but I don't want to bother him this late. With a sigh, I roll over. It can wait until tomorrow.

Chapter 11

Jacques

Monday morning, I wake up at five a.m. after a restless sleep. Yesterday was busy with Papa trying to convince me to change my mind. Despite him giving me three weeks, he is insistent on trying to change me earlier.

He also had Maman, Rémy, and Céleste involved. All four of them tried to talk me out of it, telling me I was making a mistake. Over breakfast, lunch, and dinner, we argued back and forth. They do not like that I am going to be their competitor. I take this as a sign that deep down they know I will succeed.

I never once faltered. I am seeing my new business through, and no amount of threats will change that.

When sleep evades me, I get up, change, and go jogging. The sky is dark, and the ground is wet from overnight rainfall. The morning is fresh and chillier than other mornings, which invigorates me. My feet pound the cobblestone pavement as I jog street after street, pushing myself harder and faster to rid myself of the angst from yesterday. It is a new day of a new week, and I intend to make it a good one.

At quarter to six, I stop outside a small café that opened early. Taking in my surroundings, I realise I am not far from Jane's apartment. Since I did not see her yesterday, and after the stress from my family, I need to see her. The one person who will make everything okay again.

Struck with an idea, I order two cappuccinos, two fresh croissants, and arrive at Jane's at six a.m. Darkness is disappearing with the onset of dawn, but the streets are still bathed in dull, unnatural yellow light. I press the intercom button with my elbow, but there is no answer. She is probably still asleep, so I keep pressing.

Finally, there is a click. "Do you realise what time it is?" Her voice is thick with sleep, and it is the most beautiful sound.

I grin into the camera and hold up the coffee and croissants. "*Petit déjeuner* on a budget."

There is silence at first, then, "I'm on the fifth floor, come on up," followed by a buzz and a clunk as the door unlocks.

I take the steps two at a time and knock on her door when I reach it. It flings open almost immediately. A gust of air rushes in and whips her white satin nightgown against her slim form.

"Good morning, come in," she greets with a bright grin, holding the door open wider.

Despite having just woken up, she looks stunning. Her eyes are shining and her cheeks are rosy.

I step inside and she closes the door after me, locking it.

"Just give me five minutes to shower and change." She holds up five fingers as she rushes off to the bathroom, grabbing a change of clothes from a chest of drawers along the way.

Placing the coffee and croissants on the coffee table, I move a multicoloured cushion aside, then sit on the sofa to wait. I glance around her small apartment. Everything is open plan except for the bathroom. It is comfortable. Not extravagant like my own. Despite the fact she is only here temporarily, she has made it homely.

Colourful pillows on the sofa, photos dotted around presumably of family and friends, a pile of magazines on the coffee table, and a few books on the bedside cupboard. Not much, but it has everything my apartment does not. I put my books out on Saturday, but they do very little to make it homely.

The water switches off from the bathroom, and Jane emerges a few moments later. Her long, blonde hair is hanging loosely around her shoulders. Dressed in casual slacks and a woolly jumper, she has never looked so beautiful to me. Other women I dated in the past would have their hair done, perfect makeup, and exquisite clothing, even for impromptu dates. I love that Jane is comfortable in her own skin.

It is one of the first things I noticed about her. What drew me to her.

When she sits next to me, the scent of flowers is strong, and I shuffle closer so our shoulders are touching. Reaching across for the second coffee cup, I hand it to her. Our fingers brush when she takes it, smiling brilliantly at me. Warmth spreads up my arm, making my heart race. I cannot take my eyes off her as she sips her coffee.

"What are you doing here? And so early?" She places the cup on the floor. "We have work today."

"*Oui*, we do, but not until eight thirty." Unable to resist her, I lean forward and press my lips against her soft, warm ones. She tastes of coffee, and her delicate flowery scent fills my nostrils. "I hope I did not inconvenience you by coming here so early." I sit back. "I wanted to, uh, *surprendre* you."

Some words I still struggle with. I should know the English word, as I have heard it before, but I cannot always remember. Jane never seems to mind, and I appreciate that she understands me and helps me improve.

"No, it's no inconvenience. It's a nice surprise, thank you." She grins at me. "I'm just sorry you had to see me in my nighty."

I shake my head, a slow smile spreading across my face. "I am not." I kiss her again, slow and sensual.

Does she not realise I want to know every part of her? The good, the bad, the in between.

She relaxes against me, her hands gripping my t-shirt, still slightly damp from my morning jog. This does not appear to deter her, and she does not hold back in showing me she is willing to take this further. Until her stomach lets out a loud growl and I pull away. We both laugh.

"You are hungry," I say.

"Starving."

I reach across for the croissants and remove them along with some butter and jam.

"I'll grab some plates and cutlery." Jane jumps to her feet and returns seconds later with plates and knives.

We make small talk while we eat and drink, and I find myself enjoying the small intimacies. When I am alone, I do not have anyone to talk to. Today is the first day in a long time I am not lonely. I imagine enjoying many more mornings like this. With Jane.

But how will it work?

Mentally shaking the thoughts from my head, I instead ask, "You do not wake early before work?"

Jane shrugs. "Depends. Sometimes I'll go for a walk first thing, but I had a late night thanks to my boss back in Australia, so I was *trying* to get some extra sleep." She gives me a pointed glare, and I smile innocently. I do not regret surprising her with breakfast, and she has enjoyed it, too. It has been a wonderful morning.

"We had a Zoom meeting—" Jane continues, then sighs.

I sense sadness in that sigh, and I look at her, frowning. "Are you okay?"

She shakes her head and tells me the news she received last night.

It hits me hard, and for a moment, I cannot breathe. Our time together was always going to be short, but to be even shorter...

Jane looks miserable. I do not like seeing her so upset, and I wish to make this better for her. Help her see that all is not lost.

I smile at her and take her hands, looking deep into her eyes. "It is terrible news to be sure, but that means we must make the most of the time we have together, *non?*"

In proving true to my word, I waste no time capturing her lips and kissing her with heated passion, making it clear where I want this to go. When she does not refuse, there is no holding back.

---

*M*on Dieu. I am in trouble.

Jane's soft skin is flush against mine, warm in her soft, comfortable bed. It is impossible to think of anything but this perfect moment. With my arm wrapped around her middle, she is a perfect fit. She stirs and rolls over to face me. I tighten my grip around her and pull her against me. Smiling lazily, I lean in to kiss her.

"*Bonjour beauté*," I whisper when I pull away.

A wide grin spreads across her face, and goose bumps rise on her skin. But just as quickly, it disappears again. Shadows of great sadness darken her face. I do not miss the tears in her eyes before she clears her throat and moves away, taking the covers with her. She sits on the side of the bed, her back to me.

She does not need to speak. I know what caused this sadness. I move over to her and wrap my arm around her waist, pressing my lips against her exposed shoulder. She shudders beneath my touch and slackens against me. I rest my chin on her shoulder.

She turns her head to look up at me with watery eyes, making the blue shine like the ocean. "I like you, Jack. Too much."

I frown. "You can like someone too much?"

"I think so." She shuffles around to face me. "Especially in our situation. I keep thinking how difficult it will be when I go home. How is this...*us* even going to work?"

Of course. This does not surprise me, but I do not want to worry about it now. The thought is already too painful, and I want to enjoy every possible moment with Jane. Sitting up, I adjust the sheet around my waist.

"That is six weeks away, *non*?"

"I know, but—"

I silence her with a kiss. "We should not worry about something that is not here."

When I smile, it does not feel genuine. True, I do want to enjoy our time together, but the thought of what we will both lose at the end weighs heavily on my heart.

I reach out and tuck her soft hair behind her ear. "We should enjoy our time now, *non*?"

She looks me in the eye, as though trying to read my soul. "Of course, you're right." She shakes her shoulders and grins at me. "In light of that, we must live in the moment."

"We must?"

She nods once, a twinkle in her eyes. "Let's do something. Anything. Make the most of the last few weeks together."

I am not the type of person to live in the moment, but Jane makes me want to. I even know a place I would like to take her. "Tonight we do just that."

Jane's laughter rings out, making me smile. "But that makes no sense! Living in the moment doesn't mean doing it later. It means doing it *now*."

"We must work, *non*? Claude will be unhappy if we do not show up."

Jane tuts and playfully rolls her eyes. "You're right, I suppose. But I just learned something new about you. You're practical."

I nod. I have always been this way. It is easier than being emotional.

"You are not?" I ask.

"I am when I must be. Otherwise, I like to take things as they come." She reaches over to her phone and taps the screen, gasping. "Although right now, practical is good. It's nearly eight thirty. We should have left already!"

She pushes the covers away and goes to scramble off the bed, but I grab her again and pull her back as she shrieks with laughter. I only wish I could spend the whole day listening to her beautiful laughter.

"Jack, we've got to—"

I do not let her finish and instead smother her lips, promising without words that I do not care if we are late for work.

"We can live in the moment a little bit," I say when I pull away. "But I will message Claude. Thirty minutes is not too late, *non*?" I lean back across the bed and remove my phone from my sweatpants, sending off a message.

The change in our relationship is both the best and worst thing that has happened. I cannot get enough of her. She makes me feel alive for the first time in a long time. Everything is not only perfect in the world, but I can confidently be who I want to be and not be afraid of the future.

But now, I do not want to let her go. Ever. Yet I know I must.

Chapter 12

Jane

I arrive at work at nine a.m., and Jacques is a few minutes behind me as he went home first to change. Pulling the door open, I greet a chirpy, "*Bonjour*," and hang my coat up. A few people return the greeting, even Francine. Claude is nowhere in sight. Is he *still* in hiding?

Oh, well, I'll talk to him later. Nothing can ruin my mood this morning. I leave my drawers unlocked, too, giving Francine the benefit of the doubt. Just because we don't get on doesn't mean she's going to steal anything. What if she genuinely *did* want a pen?

As if on cue, Francine appears beside my desk.

"*Bonjour*, Jane, you are looking very nice today." She gives me a once-over.

This compliment catches me off-guard because she always looks down her nose at me. But today, she's giving me a genuine smile. Then again, she might appear genuine because I'm in a stupidly good mood. Didn't Regina say I was glowing the other night? Oh hell, is it really that obvious?

"Oh, uh, thanks," I stammer with a smile. "Um, did you need something?"

I feel like I should give a compliment back. You know how when someone compliments you and your instinct is to give one back? Well, I'm trying to do better at not doing that. I mean, Francine *doesn't* look nice today. She's in her usual mini skirt and blouse that shows too much cleavage. Is it so difficult to dress her age? So, since I was always taught to only say what I mean, I'm keeping silent.

Thankfully she doesn't seem to expect a reply and instead asks, "I need to borrow the company credit card. Claude asked me to buy some supplies." She thrusts a piece of paper at me.

Rattled and slightly suspicious—I can't help it—I take the paper from her and scan it over. A printed email from Claude to Francine with the request. It says to see me for the credit card. I can't help being uneasy, but if Claude trusts her, I need to trust *him*.

I'll confirm with him later, but for now I'll give Francine the benefit of the doubt.

"All right." I hand the paper back to her. I grab the credit card and hand it over. When she goes to take it, I instinctively grip tighter than I should.

She frowns at me, and I laugh nervously, finally loosening my grip. She nods once and goes back to her desk.

"I will go out this morning. I will not be back until after lunch."

I breathe out and nod. "No worries, just give the credit card back when you're done. And please don't forget the receipts."

She nods, then sits, and I turn back to my desk. I'm all jittery and nervous, so I take a deep breath and release it slowly.

Everything is okay. She showed me proof. I'll confirm with Claude later. I'm just being paranoid.

As my anxiety eases, my good mood comes back, and I start humming as I power on the computer. Everything disappears from my mind as I think about my morning with Jacques.

I won't lie, I was initially annoyed at being woken up at such an ungodly hour, until I realised who it was, then all my annoyance disappeared. *So* worth it. Although now all I can think of is hearing him say, "Hello, beautiful," in French to me every morning.

This is bad.

I don't regret a thing, but everything will become super complicated. My mind is wandering into dangerous territory, thinking about an impossible future. Not caring about the broken heart I'm going to wear at the end. There's something special about Jacques DuPont. Not only do I want to know everything about him, I'm also eager to see if we have a future.

Now that I've slept on Regina's news, and spoken to Jacques about it, I'm certain six weeks is enough time to figure it out. For now, I'm going to sit back and enjoy the ride.

The door opens and a cool breeze rushes in. I glance around as Jacques enters dressed in his usual fancy suit and shiny shoes. His hair is styled into its signature coif, and I find myself wishing I could run my fingers through its soft thickness again.

After greeting the office, he casts a glance around, lingering on me long enough to send an inconspicuous wink my way before striding to his office. I melt in my chair, a large grin spreading across my face.

When I log in, I remember that Jacques never told me what I owe him on dry cleaning. I send him an instant message to remind him.

I sigh happily. This is by far the best start to a Monday ever. I might have to encourage more breakfasts on a budget.

Jacques sends a message back.

Non, you do not. You owe me nothing but your lovely company.

A silly grin spreads across my face, and I send back a blowing-kiss emoji, then focus on work. If I had a choice, I'd spend all day sending flirty messages with Jacques. Claude *definitely* wouldn't like that.

The next couple of hours fly by, and the smile on my face barely wavers. Even when I read through Regina's contract and sign it, sending it back to her and Claude, it doesn't falter. I've accepted it, and nothing else matters right now.

I'm convinced nothing can shift this mood, until I see Claude dash to his office without a glance at me and close the door. He hasn't greeted me, either! If this isn't proof that he's avoiding me, I don't know what is.

Claude's door opens again at midday, so now is as good a time as any to clear the air. This is getting silly. I mean, he received a text from Jacques saying we'll be late, and he doesn't say a thing? That is *so* not Claude's style.

Saving my work, I stand and stride to his office. I peer in to find Claude with his head down, reading a document on his desk. I knock on the doorframe, and he looks up, his face paling.

"Oh. Jane, hi." His cheeks turn pink, and he averts his gaze. "What can I do for you?"

Oh no, we're not doing professional right now. I step into his office and close the door. Claude swallows, his Adam's apple moving up and down his throat.

No point in dragging this out, so I jump straight in. "I signed the amended contract and sent it back to you and Regina."

Claude's face crumples, the professional demeanour disappearing. This situation must be difficult for him, too. I never stopped to think he may feel the same way as me. After all, we've become close friends, and it won't be the same not seeing each other every day.

"I'm sorry I didn't tell you." He clears his throat, but I hear the wobble in his voice. "It was decided late last week when we reviewed the budget. I wanted to speak to Regina first, in case she could do anything."

"Clearly she couldn't." I sit on a chair opposite him.

He shakes his head. "I'm so sorry, Jane. I hate to do this, but there is no other option. Budgetary restraints and all that. Losing one contractor will allow us to hire two more staff members, one part time and one full time, and we'll *still* be saving money."

Even though I've come to terms with it, it still stings to talk about it. "I understand." I force a smile. "I don't blame you, Claude."

Relief floods his face. "You don't?"

"Of course not, why would I?"

He shrugs. "Penny's going to be upset when I tell her."

I cringe at the thought. "You haven't told her yet?"

"Of course not, that's not fair on you."

I smile despite myself. That's so typical of Claude. Always doing things the right way so as not to hurt anyone. Which is why I know this is difficult for him.

The silence becomes awkward between us, but there's no more to say. My contract was always going to end; it just came sooner than planned. Nothing anyone can do about it.

With a sigh, I stand and step to the side away from the chair. "I need to get back to work, but are we all good? Will you stop avoiding me now? Don't think I didn't notice."

Claude stands with a guilty smile and comes around to me. "I'm sorry, I didn't intend to avoid you. I was worried if I spoke to you, I'd spill everything before the time was right."

That makes sense. "I understand, but no more cold shoulders. And don't be a stranger, okay? I want you, Penny, and Amélie in my life always."

Claude freezes. "You sound like you're leaving now. You're not, are you? Quitting, that is?"

I stare at him, agape. "No, of course not! I'm trying to put a positive spin on an otherwise unfortunate situation. Besides, you received Jacques' text this morning. Why would I rush off now?"

Claude breaks out into his signature, playful grin. "Oh yes, I have a lot to say about that." He looks at his watch and winces. "But it'll have to wait as I've got a report to do by lunch time."

With a nod, I leave his office, and a weight lifts off my shoulders. With that sorted, it's time to focus on making the most of my time in Paris.

I'm going to make sure it's the *best* six weeks ever.

Chapter 13

Jane

I glance up from my computer screen when someone clears their throat next to my desk. Francine is standing there with a handbag over her shoulder. Is it that time already? A quick glance and my computer screen confirms it's five p.m.

"Francine, hi."

Today has been a pretty good day for Francine and me. I think we've finally reached the point of being civilised adults.

"*Salut,* Jane. *Merci* for the loan of the credit card." She removes the card and receipts from her bag and puts everything on my desk.

Crap! I totally forgot to confirm with Claude if the email was legit. I just hope like hell I *am* being paranoid, and everything is fine.

"I would like to buy you a coffee." Francine doesn't meet my gaze. "Tomorrow morning, at Café de Paris." She shuffles awkwardly from foot to foot in her heels.

I stare at her agog. Where is this coming from? We've never had coffee together. Ever. When I don't immediately respond, she looks at me with a smile verging on a cringe. If she detests me so much, why is she asking?

Tongue-tied, I mumble something unintelligible before settling for, "Uh, sure. Shall we meet at eight?"

Francine's smile is a little less cringey now and more natural. "Yes, eight is fine." She turns to leave, pauses, then turns back. "I will buy you coffee. To apologise." She practically races out of the office.

I'm left sitting at my desk, dumbstruck. Well...that was unexpected. Francine apologising? Old me would've been suspicious, wondering what she's up to. Loved-up me is sure she's genuine. Since she's been given a warning, maybe she's trying to do things right this time.

Shaking myself out of my shocked state, I put the credit card away and keep my bag on the desk so I can pack up. I put the receipts aside to scan and send to the accounts team tomorrow.

Claude appears at my desk a few minutes later.

"Francine just offered to buy me coffee tomorrow," I muse as I shut my computer down and stand. "As an apology, apparently."

"That's good, isn't it?" Claude rests his arm on the top of the wall of the pod. "She's trying to make an effort."

"True, it was a surprise, that's all."

Claude takes out his phone and starts tapping the screen, probably messaging Penny. Speaking of, I owe her a reply from a message she sent earlier.

Picking up my handbag, I slip the strap over my shoulder as I ask, "By the way, you definitely *did* ask Francine to borrow my credit card so she could buy supplies today, right?"

Claude doesn't answer straight away, transfixed by something on his phone. He's grinning at his screen, and I can hear a baby giggle. It must be a video from Penny.

"Claude?"

His head snaps up, and he blinks a couple of times. "Oh yeah, all good."

Not convinced he heard me, I'm about to ask him again, but Jacques emerges from his office, stealing my attention. As he approaches my desk, his eyes train on me, and he smiles broadly.

Claude says something, but I don't hear a thing. All I can focus on are dark, hooded eyes, and one hell of a sexy smile, dimples on full display. Jacques stops next to me and doesn't delay in swooping in for a quick, heated kiss. The type that sends my pulse racing and my knees weakening.

My head spins when Jacques pulls away, and I draw in much-needed air. A smug, satisfied smile settles on his face, and I breathe out slowly, willing my racing heart to slow down. A silly smile stretches across my lips.

"Guys, really?"

I turn to Claude, who's completely red faced. Maybe the kiss was hotter than I realised. My face warms at the thought, and I fan myself with my hand, making both Jacques and Claude laugh.

"We better not do that at the office again," I say, slightly breathless.

"I agree," Claude says. "I'm all for you two getting together, but keep personal stuff away from work."

His tone is serious, but he's smiling. A quick glance around confirms we're the only three here, which is a relief. Claude knowing our relationship status is one thing, but there's no reason for anyone else to know.

Jacques says nothing, only nods like he doesn't have a care in the world.

"Well, I'm going home," Claude announces. "Can you two lock up?"

I nod. Claude leaves with a wave and a "*bonne nuit*" over his shoulder.

Jacques and I go around the office, turning off the lights and making sure all electrical equipment is switched off.

We step outside a few minutes later, a chilly breeze slapping me in the face. I shiver as I wrap my scarf around my neck, then shrug my coat on, buttoning it up. I watch in envy as Jacques puts his gloves on, chiding myself for forgetting mine this morning. Folding my arms over my chest, I stick my hands under my armpits to keep them warm.

I swear it wasn't this cold when I went out to lunch. I haven't checked the forecast for ages, but I look above and see dark clouds are threatening rain. Damn. I hope it doesn't ruin our evening.

"You are cold?" Jacques observes, turning from the door after locking it and slipping his arm across my shoulders.

"A little, but I'm okay."

Jacques glances at the sky and tuts. "I hope it does not rain."

"Hey, we're living in the moment, right?" I grin up at him. "We'll deal with it."

"*Oui,* you are right." He pulls me to his side and plants a tender kiss on my temple. "You like walking, *non*?"

"Of course! Where are we going?"

"First we go home and change." Jacques steers me away from the office in the direction of his car. "You have walking shoes? I would like to take you to a special place."

"No, I wear heels when I walk," I retort with a sarcastic lilt and an eye roll for effect.

Jacques doesn't seem to catch on, though. He stops and stares at me, frowning. "You do? Heels will hurt your feet."

I sigh dramatically and laugh. "You're so easy, Jack!"

His frown deepens. "Easy?" His eyes widen. "I am *not* easy. You are the first person I have been with for a long time."

By now his face is red, and I splutter and choke, coughing and laughing at the same time. It's good to know I suppose, but trust Jacques to misunderstand me.

"What is so funny?" Jacques sounds offended.

I pull myself together and explain. "Not *that* kind of easy. I mean, I appreciate the confidence boost," I grin at him, "but I mean 'easy' in the sense that you're easy to tease."

His face returns to its natural colour, and he lets out a short, surprised laugh. "You are a very unusual woman."

I lean up to place a lingering kiss on his cheek. He turns to meet my lips, and it turns slow and seductive.

"Of *course*, I've got walking shoes," I say when we pull apart, my heart racing. "I don't like walking in heels if I can help it."

Jacques shakes his head, and we start walking again. "You and your Australian expressions."

"You love it." I grin, a fissure of excitement coursing through me.

I can feel Jacques' gaze on me, and when I look across at him, his gaze is intense, and he's smiling softly. "I do."

I shiver again, this time not from the cold. Something changes between us. I'm not sure what, but we're closer somehow. Jacques squeezes me, then removes his arm when we stop at his car.

Once in the car, Jacques starts it and puts the heat on for me. I smile my thanks and hold my frozen hands in front of the vents.

Before driving off, Jacques turns to me and cups my cheek. "You are truly *magnifique*, Jane. You are not like other women I know."

"Well," my laugh is nervous, "I'm Australian for starters."

"*Oui*, you are." His gaze softens, and he leans in to kiss me, soft and slow with a promise of...*something*. "*Je crois que je suis en train de tomber amoureux de toi.*" He blinks, startled, and turns back to the steering wheel, putting the car in gear.

I stare at him, breathing heavily, hating that I didn't understand him. He said it quickly, too, so I didn't catch any familiar words. What startled him so much? The car moves forward, and I settle in my seat, putting my seatbelt on.

"I'm sorry, I didn't understand what you said." My cheeks are burning.

Jacques only smiles and shakes his head. "It was nothing important."

Why does it feel like it was?

Chapter 14

Jacques

While Jane is inside her apartment changing, I sit in the car outside, hands gripping the steering wheel. My mind is racing, and I am mortified I let my guard down.

What was I thinking telling her I thought I was falling in love with her? It is not a lie. It is the strongest emotion I have ever experienced. But to speak it aloud? I must be losing my senses. I am just relieved Jane does not understand French well.

As I breathe slowly to calm my racing heart, I am once again transported back to the time when Aimée was my au pair. I do not know why she has come to my mind in recent days. I had not thought of her for many years before now. Meeting Jane opened a part of my mind and heart that were dormant for so long. The parts Aimée nurtured when Maman did not.

Now, I can hear Aimée's soft, sweet voice telling me it is okay to feel and show emotion. Something I have not done for a long time.

I remember the night clearly. Maman and Papa had sent me to my bedroom when I was upset over my *grand-mère's* death. Aimée had come to comfort me and told me it was okay to be sad. I cried and cried for many hours until I fell asleep with my head on her lap.

Two weeks later, Aimée got sick and left, never to return. I was sad when she left, too, and Maman told me I was immature and stupid. I will never forget that moment as that was when I learned how to hide my emotions.

It has been many years, and it is instinct to hide behind a smile or remark. But somehow, Jane is gradually, unknowingly, demolishing the wall holding these emotions in. How can I *not* feel when she is here? She is so carefree, I wish I could be the same. I do not want to be a robot anymore.

As if on cue, the large blue door of her apartment building opens. Jane slips out wrapped up in a thick coat, scarf, and gloves. I cannot deny the cold weather is unexpected. She catches my gaze through the window and sends me a brilliant smile. My heart stutters, and that feeling of love overwhelms me again.

Maybe I should embrace it.

When Jane is in the car, I drive back to my apartment and dash inside to change and pack the food I prepared during my lunch break. Conceding it is cold enough to wrap up, I bring my own gloves and scarf, too.

We arrive at our destination at six p.m. We are standing in front of a lattice archway covered in ivy, leading to a walking path. Jane is looking around in awe. I slide my arm across her shoulders and hold her close, relishing in her warmth.

The late evening sun peeks out from the clouds on the horizon before disappearing seconds later. I look up at the dark grey clouds, which are darker and heavier now. I thought it might rain earlier, but now I think we might get snow. A walk in the snow sounds wonderful.

"This is *la promenade plantée*," I explain to Jane. "It is a walkway on an old elevated railway line. It is just over four kilometres long."

Moving my arm from across her shoulders, I take my gloves and scarf out of my backpack. After wrapping my scarf around my neck, I slip the gloves on my hands, put my backpack on, then take Jane's gloved hand in my own. We walk through the archway, entering a narrow pathway lined with trees, shrubs, and flowers.

The scent of lavender catches on the breeze the same moment we enter an area with lavender plants on either side, purple flowers bright and vibrant. The sun makes an appearance at the same moment, dapples of light appearing along the ground before disappearing again.

A glance through the trees to the horizon shows the gap in the clouds closing for good, with no way for the sun to reappear tonight.

"This is so beautiful," Jane whispers, as though she fears the beauty will disappear if she talks too loudly.

I cannot disagree. White blossoms hang from trees with bright green leaves. Pink, white, and yellow flowers are dotted in the garden beds and on some bushes. I have been here a couple of times but never truly appreciated its beauty.

"There is more to see," I say, gently tugging on her hand. "Let us keep walking."

We do so and follow the pathway that is as far as the eye can see, lined with plant life the entire way. There are other people around, too, enjoying the diminishing daylight before day turns to night and the weather changes. Rain or snow, whatever it ends up being.

Other couples walking hand-in-hand pass us, along with some joggers, dog walkers, and parents with prams.

We follow the pathway, not talking at first, just enjoying the scenery. When the pathway curves, there are more lavender plants, and the scent is stronger as a breeze whips through the bushes. I stop and pick a lavender flower off its stem. Turning to Jane, I smile at her as I tuck it behind her ear before kissing her briefly. Are her feelings as strong as mine?

Her closed eyes and soft smile confirms it is not just me experiencing this. Her eyes flutter open and our gazes meet. She smiles and kisses me one last time before urging me to continue walking.

We walk under another ivy-covered archway into a small courtyard where there are two iron benches on either side. Another memory of coming here with Aimée many years ago flashes in my mind, and I stop abruptly. So much changes over time, but this courtyard has mostly stayed the same. The benches have been repainted, the plants have grown, the buildings around us are more decrepit, but the image of us sitting on one of those benches together is imprinted on my brain.

It was springtime, like now, and she had handed me a small cup of hot chocolate. I remember thinking it was the best hot chocolate I had ever drank. I was only ten, and I have had much better since, but at such a young age anything new is "the best." I say something, which I no longer remember, but she laughs. She always had a beautiful, melodious laugh. But that laughter quickly changed to a hacking cough.

She fumbled in a bag for a tissue and coughed into it for so long, I worried she might hurt herself. Eventually she stopped, and I saw blood on the tissue. She was quick to reassure me it was nothing to worry about and promised it would pass.

Of course, I was too young to know better, and I believed her. This was our last outing together as she called in sick the next day and never returned.

Now that I am letting myself feel emotion again, the memory of Aimée is crippling. I wish I was older back then, old enough to understand that she was very sick so I could have asked Maman or Papa to visit her one last time. While not confirmed, I realise now she must have died. I could ask my parents, but there is no point. They will probably say they do not remember her.

There's a gentle hand on my arm, and Jane tentatively asks, "Are you okay?"

I blink a few times, realising moisture has gathered in my eyes. I look into her concerned face, and my cheeks turn warm. There is no way she would not have seen that emotional display, yet strangely I am not embarrassed. I would rather show my feelings around Jane.

And so, I tell her about my au pair, and Jane listens without judgement, only compassion, her arm linked through mine.

"I'm so sorry, Jack," Jane says softly when we begin walking again past the benches. "That must've been very difficult for you."

I smile at her. "You do not need to be sorry, but *merci* for listening." I pause before adding, "I apologise if I do not always show emotion. It is not always easy for me."

Jane squeezes my arm and smiles at me. "I understand, and I will never push you, but I want you to know I will never judge you. I love a man who is not afraid to show how he feels." She gives me a cheeky grin, and my heart warms.

"*Merci*, Jane."

For a few minutes, we continue walking, talking occasionally before coming out into an open area. We are high up on a bridge now, the streets lined with trees and old buildings. The buildings are in various states of decay. Balconies on all levels, some with pot plants, others with clothes drying, and others with nothing but a table setting.

We keep walking, following a path past residential apartment buildings for a few metres before going back onto a path lined with greenery again. We walk for about half an hour before coming to an open picnic-style area. Lots of benches, trees, and a kiosk.

"Are you hungry?" I ask.

"Starving. Shall we grab something from the kiosk?" Jane points to it.

I wrinkle my nose, shaking my head. "You taught me to eat on a budget, *non*?"

She nods, and I remove my backpack.

"Come on." I gesture to a free bench where we go and sit.

I remove a thermos of hot coffee and two rolls wrapped in plastic wrap. I hand her one of the rolls and place another next to me before pouring us both a drink.

She takes the coffee and sips, moaning in appreciation. "Thank you. You bought all this today?"

I give her a cheeky smile. "I went home at lunch to prepare everything. I had the idea this morning."

She jabs me in the side with her elbow. "So much for living in the moment."

I pick up my roll and peel back the plastic, biting into the roll. An array of flavours come to life—tuna mixed with the freshness of salad, the vinegar of mustard, the acid from tomatoes, and saltiness of anchovies and olives. "I like to know what I am doing," I confess after I swallow.

"True, I guess I'm the same. It's called being organised, I guess." Jane peels the plastic back on her own roll.

"Exactly."

Jane bites into her roll and chews. "This is delicious. What is it?"

"*Pan bagnat,*" I answer.

She looks at me blankly and laughs. "I have no idea what it is, but you're a legendary sandwich maker. Is this as far as your cooking repertoire goes?"

I shake my head. "*Non,* this is something I, how do you Australians say it? 'Whip together' at a moment's notice."

"Nice one, Jack." She takes another bite and chews. "So, you can cook?"

"*Oui,* I enjoy cooking." I think for a moment, struck with an idea. "Will you let me cook for you?"

Her eyes widen, and she nods. "I would love that."

We go back to eating, but a few minutes later, Jane groans. "No, don't rain!"

I look up and grin at the tiny snowflakes falling. "*Sacrebleu!*" I jump to my feet, roll discarded. "*Il neige!*"

Jane gasps and is soon standing beside me. "Oh my gosh!" She holds out her arms as snowflakes cover her hair, face, and clothes.

People around us stop to enjoy the snowfall also, chatting excitedly and taking photos. After an unseasonably warm winter, I did not expect snow in April.

My attention is taken away from the falling snow by Jane's happy laughter. I turn to her where she is spinning around in glee, covered in tiny snowflakes. By her reaction, I assume she has never seen snow before, and it is the most beautiful sight.

She stops spinning and turns to me with a giggle, stumbling from dizziness. I go up to her and wrap my arms around her, holding her tight. She turns in my arms and faces me, wrapping her arms around my neck. When we lean in to kiss, snow falling around us, I cannot imagine a more magical moment.

Chapter 15

A

Jane

As beautiful as it is, it gets cold quickly. I take some photos, then we grab our things and head back, finishing our food while we walk.

It's dark when we arrive at Jacques' car and the falling snow is illuminated by the light from a lamp post. I stop at the passenger door, and Jacques steps closer, gently pushing me against the metal body of the car. He leans in to kiss me, softly at first, but it quickly turns passionate.

"Would you like to come back to my place?" he asks when we pull back for air, resting his forehead on mine. His dark eyes are glinting in promise.

My heart leaps, and I nod. A chance to see where he lives? How can I refuse?

We arrive at his building and waste no time getting out of the cold. Inside his apartment, he pins me to the door, kissing me again, nothing held back. The dynamics change between us. Everything is so much *more*. More intense. More desirable. Every single emotion is so strong, I want to burst. When Jacques pulls back and takes my hand to lead me to his room, I realise with overwhelming clarity that I have fallen for Jacques DuPont.

*

The next morning, I wake early from a deep and extremely comfortable sleep. I recall the clarity of my thoughts from last night, and the realisation hits me hard all over again. My heart does a little flip. All night I dreamed about kissing in the snow. Even in the dream, I could still feel the snowflakes landing on my face in cool little needle pricks.

I'm a goner. I fear I'll never return emotionally from this.

My heart is racing, and I push the worrisome thoughts aside. Closing my eyes again, I breathe in deeply and hold it, focusing on where I am. If I can get a sense of time and place, it'll help calm me down.

Soft, memory-foam mattress. Silky sheets, probably with an insanely high thread count. A featherdown quilt and matching pillows. Add a bonus strong arm holding me close to an even stronger body...

Jacques' apartment.

Okay, this is good. My heart rate slows, and I release my breath.

I roll onto my back, stretching my body from my fingers to my toes. Jacques stirs and rolls over but doesn't wake. Not wanting to disturb him, I lay there for a moment, enjoying the comfort. I don't remember *ever* sleeping on a mattress so heavenly. I slept like a baby and didn't wake once.

When my bladder twinges, I push the covers back and sit up, my feet touching soft, plush carpet. There's no chill in the air like there would be in my apartment. Central heating, of course.

Spotting the door into the ensuite across from me, I get out of bed, grab my clothes off the floor, and dash across to it. I half expect my feet to freeze when they hit the bathroom tiles, but they don't. They're *warm*. This is insane. Every inch of this place is warm and comfortable.

After closing the door, I spot a second door on the far wall leading out to the rest of the apartment. Placing my clothes on the edge of the two-person corner spa, I go to the toilet and sigh in relief.

The bathroom is modern in black, grey, and splashes of white. A two-person shower with a large showerhead promises an amazing experience. The vanity spans across one wall with a mirror of the same length, two sinks, and plenty of cupboard space.

Flushing the toilet, I change and step back into the bedroom. Grabbing my phone from the bedside cupboard, I check the time. Six forty-five a.m. Still enough time to go home, get ready for work, and meet Francine.

Before waking Jacques, I take the opportunity to explore his apartment, knowing he won't mind. The bedroom follows the modern black-and-white theme from the bathroom, but with splashes of red in decorative pillows, and thick cream curtains hiding the floor-to-ceiling window taking up the entire far wall.

In the main part of the penthouse, the entire southern wall is floor-to-ceiling windows, like in his bedroom, with the same style curtains but in pale yellow. Hanging my coat, scarf, and gloves on the back of a chair, I go across to open the curtain.

The apartment is bathed in the dull morning light, and I'm greeted with a breathtaking view of Paris. The Eiffel Tower stands tall and proud high above the seemingly never-ending streets of multi-storey buildings. Everything is white, covered in snow after last night's snowfall.

Turning my back to the window, I observe the open plan kitchen-dining-lounge. Again, black and white is the theme with more use of white and splashes of black, purple, and yellow. The layout is similar to my apartment, only much bigger, more modern, and more lavish.

The kitchen is to die for with a massive island for preparing food and eating. There are stools on one side, facing the kitchen. A great way to socialise while cooking. The stove and oven are high-end, suitable for a chef. If Jacques enjoys cooking, this makes sense.

As I investigate the cupboards, fridge, and pantry, I'm pleasantly surprised to learn he's not like other bachelors. The fridge and pantry are stocked with all the normal staples, but he's got a variety of salads, vegetables, fruits, and yoghurt. Of course, I don't miss the variety of cheeses on offer, and the treats of crisps and chocolate in the pantry.

In the lounge is a comfortable-looking four-seater corner sofa facing a wall with plenty of shelves jam packed with books, and a space in the middle for the wall-mounted sixty-inch TV.

Jacques is a reader? Nice to know. I don't read as often as I'd like, but I enjoy it. Checking out the book collection, I see a lot of thriller and mystery novels, with a handful of fantasy thrown in. Interestingly, they're written in English, which I'm impressed by. Textbooks and an old encyclopaedia collection, written in French, fill up the remaining shelves. I pick out one of the encyclopaedias, surprised that the cover is in such good condition, but the pages are brittle. Realising how old they are, and I should handle with care, I put it back carefully.

Turning so my back is to the bookcase, I survey the whole open plan area. I'm not sure what, but something about this room doesn't suit Jacques. I still don't know him that well, but the glimpses I've had into his personality, he doesn't seem the type to splurge on such lavishness. So far, the only thing that remotely "looks" like him is the collection of books.

But I could be way off. What if this only proves how much I *don't* know about him?

Deep down, I don't believe that. I haven't seen him splash his money about, even taking my advice about living on a budget. Things he's said also, about not liking his privileged life. He's rich by birth, not by choice, and something in this apartment shows that. Almost like this was expected of him but not what he wanted.

With a sigh, I turn and go back into the bedroom. I pull on the curtains, where the Paris view continues, the Eiffel Tower now off centre and to the left.

"It is a *magnifique* view, *non*?"

I yelp in fright and spin around. Jacques is sitting up in bed and sends me a sleepy smile. His hair is mussed from sleep, and there are adorable lines on the side of his face from the creases of his pillow.

"Stunning," I breathe, turning back to the view. Snow is falling again, flakes drifting lazily past the window and gathering on the windowsill.

A moment later, Jacques comes up behind me and wraps his arms around my waist. I spin around in his arms and lean in to kiss him. "Good morning."

His arms tighten around me as he smiles, his eyes sparkling. "It is a very good morning. I will make you a coffee."

When he steps away, I notice he's just in his boxers. He's pleasing on the eye, mildly defined with a visible six-pack but not ripped, and a light smattering of hair across his chest. He keeps fit but not to insane levels. I could happily stand here ogling him forever.

Aware of the time, I reluctantly say, "I'd love one, but I need to go." Jacques looks disappointed so I hasten to add, "I told Francine I'd meet her this morning. I need to go so I can shower and change."

He nods. "*Oui*, I understand." He frowns, goes to say something, but then doesn't.

"Is something wrong?"

"You and Francine, you do not get on?"

I shrug. "We never used to, but we're working on it."

He thinks for a moment. "She cannot be," his brow furrows, and he looks at me as though hoping I can give him the word, "*de confiance.*"

"Trusted," I offer with a nod, "and I know. Well, I *did*. I mean, since she's been given a warning, she's changed."

Jacques' brow is creased in worry, like he doesn't entirely believe me. "You think so?"

I shrug one shoulder. "I can't say I'm convinced, but I've spent too long doubting her. Yesterday she offered me an olive branch, and I took it. Everyone deserves a second chance, right?"

The worry doesn't completely leave Jacques' face, but he smiles easier when he takes my hand and squeezes it. "You are a very good person, Jane. You will be careful, *non*?"

I nod and stroke his cheek. "I always am."

"*Bien*. I will change, then I drive you home."

"No, it's okay. I can walk." When he goes to protest, I quickly add, "I wouldn't mind a walk in the snow, and it's not far. Really, it's fine."

He relents. "*D'accord*, but tonight I would like to cook for you, and you must stay the night again."

"Oh, must I?" I raise an eyebrow and place my hands on my hips.

Jacques opens his mouth to speak, then closes it and narrows his eyes. "You are teasing, *non*?"

I grin and drop my arms. "Of course I am. You're learning!"

Jacques laughs, then in a soft, almost embarrassed voice, adds, "I am not so alone with you here."

My breath catches at this confession, and I learn a whole lot about Jacques in just a few short words. He's just as lonely as I've been in the past. And that, to me, speaks volumes.

"Then nothing will stop me."

I kiss him goodbye and leave. When I exit the building onto the pavement, the door closing behind me, I nearly run into a well-dressed couple standing in front of the intercom. I gasp and stumble back against the door.

"Oh, I'm so sorry!"

The couple look at me but say nothing. They're middle-aged and extremely well-dressed. One glance at the man and there is no mistaking who he is, even though I've never met him before in my life.

Jacques' father. Older and greyer, but he's got the same angled jawline and brown eyes, not to mention that natural confidence that seems to run in the family. He's dressed in a similar style of suit Jacques usually wears, with a long black coat.

The woman must be his mother, but she is much more petite. With makeup perfectly applied, she's wearing a black fur hat that matches her black mink coat with a silver fur collar and cuffs.

What the hell are they even doing here at seven a.m.? Do they never sleep?

Neither of us speaks, but they don't hide their distaste as they scrutinise me from head to toe, probably judging me for wearing yesterday's clothes. *Cheap* clothes at that. Do they even know who I am? Has Jacques told them about me?

Geez, the DuPonts are way out of my league, and this only widens the divide between Jacques and me. How the hell will I ever fit into his world?

Tongue tied and flustered, I throw them a brief apologetic smile, then push past and rush off toward home.

⁓⁕⁓

The random encounter never leaves my mind, and the uncertainty of my life in Jacques' world never goes away. The only thing that silences it is focusing on getting home and ready for work.

The overnight snowfall is all over social media and local news outlets. Apparently, it's the first time in years to have such a cold snap at this time of year, so the hype is warranted.

After showering and changing, I make my way downstairs at seven-thirty a.m. I'm early, but my plan is to take my time getting to the café so I can enjoy the snow.

While it isn't very thick, it covers the ground, trees, rooftops, and cars. I never knew so much white could be so beautiful. The cool breeze slaps me in the face, and I shiver.

The snow crunches under my feet as I start walking, snowflakes falling and covering my jacket and hair. I look up at the dark, grey clouds, noticing how different they are to normal rain clouds. They're heavier and darker.

I wander the streets, past the multi-storey buildings; the fresh air is cool and scented with baking bread and croissants. My breath comes out in a puff of smoke each time I breathe out.

Reaching the café a few minutes early, I find a bench, brush the snow away, and sit down to wait. Despite the cold, there's something magical about sitting in the snow while it falls around me. I take a few photos and send them back home to my friends and parents. Since it's still early evening over there, a few people reply, and we text back and forth for a few minutes.

I text Jacques, too, who confirms it *was* his parents who I nearly barrelled over. Turns out his father came with a business proposition. Offered to step down as CEO of Entreprises DuPont and let Jacques take the position, but only if he gave up Solutions Exécutives.

Jacques said no.

I am so bloody proud, and every time I think about it, my heart swells with love for this man. He's proving day by day that he wants to make a difference and do what *he* wants. It would be no easy feat.

Yet that divide between us feels like a canyon now. His family will always be there, and I'm never going to fit. Not me, Plain Jane.

My phone vibrates in my hand, and I look down to see another reply from Mum. Dad will sometimes message, but usually it's Mum. He's just not that tech savvy.

Despite how much I'm enjoying life overall in Paris now, I still miss everyone back home. Just not as much as I did. I'm looking forward to seeing them again, but I'm also in no rush for the next few weeks to speed by. In fact, a part of me is hoping Regina will find another job for me. Or maybe I'll find one myself. I didn't want to leave initially, but I'd do anything for Jacques. I could go home for a holiday, then come back to Paris.

Or more specifically, I don't want to go anywhere without Jacques. And if this thing between us turns serious, we need to talk about it. Not yet, though. Way too soon. Besides, I need to settle these ridiculous thoughts that I don't fit into Jacques' life. Perhaps talking to him about it will help. Love can conquer all, right?

I still have no idea what Jacques said in the car last night, but my gut tells me it was something big. Something even *he* felt was too soon to say. If that's the case, he can't know my thoughts. Not yet.

"Why are you sitting out in the snow?"

I jump and look up. Francine is standing in front of me. Today she's more her age. Her makeup is more natural. Gone is the mini skirt, high heels, and skimpy top. Instead, she's wearing black trousers and boots, and rugged up in a coat, gloves, and scarf. I can't see what sort of blouse she's wearing, but dare I say it? She looks *good.*

"You look lovely today, Francine." I throw her a smile so she knows I'm genuine.

Her eyes widen, and her cheeks gain a slight pink tinge, but she remains stoic.

"And anyway," I continue, answering her question, "it's lovely sitting in the snow. I've never seen it before last night."

Francine stares at me, mouth gaping open. "Have you not?"

I stand. "I'm from Australia, remember? And where I'm from, it never snows. On the rare really cold winter, the hills might get a few flakes, but nothing like this." I hold my arms out and do a single spin, giggling.

"You are embarrassing yourself." Francine sniffs and sticks her nose in the air. "Let us have coffee."

She storms off and into the café. I shake my head and grudgingly follow. So much for an apology coffee. Francine will always be Francine, I suppose.

When I step inside, the café is empty apart from Francine, who's already placed the order and is waiting. She hasn't asked me what I want, but I say nothing. It's the thought that counts after all, right?

"I ordered you a latte," Francine says matter-of-factly.

I stop myself from wrinkling my nose just in time and smile instead. "Thank you."

Truth is, I prefer cappuccinos because they're stronger. Lattes are too weak.

Francine digs into her handbag and pulls out a long, rectangular box wrapped in white paper with silver stars. She hesitates before holding it out to me. I look at it for a long moment, then back up at her with a frown. I don't get to say anything before she shoves it into my hand, and I have no choice but to wrap my fingers around it.

"But—"

The barista calls out Francine's name, and she steps forward to grab the coffee. Handing me one of the cups, she steps back and nods.

"My job is done." Her smile is tight. "I will meet you at the office."

Head held high, she breezes out of the café.

"Uh, thanks," I call after her, but I'm not sure if she hears me.

With coffee in one hand and the gift in the other, I stare at the door, unable to fully comprehend what just happened. With a shake of my head, I step outside and place both items on the table. Unwrapping the gift, I shove the paper into my bag, then open the box. A gold necklace glistens up at me with a pendant of the Eiffel Tower on it.

Pretty and expensive. I love it, but if it's meant to be an apology gift, it's a bloody expensive one. I'm not sure if there's an ulterior motive. Does she expect something in return? Well, sorry, Francine, but I never asked for this. I'm not going to spend hundreds of euros on her. In fact, I don't think I can take it.

Something is off, I just don't know what. Call me ungrateful, but I trust my gut, and it's screaming at me. Jacques' warning to be careful has stuck in my mind. I don't want to go back to being super paranoid, but I can be on my guard.

So, shoving the box in my bag, I pick up my coffee and go to work.

When I arrive at the office, I hang up my coat, scarf, and gloves as Francine says from behind me, "Jane dear, may I borrow the company credit card again?"

I frown and turn to her. "Again?"

She gives a single nod, her face expressionless, and holds out a piece of paper. I take it. Another email from Claude confirming he's approved her to use the credit card to buy the items.

I glance at his office, thinking I should confirm with him properly this time, but he's not in yet.

As if reading my thoughts, Francine cuts in, "I must go out right away. You are running a training session this afternoon, correct? Claude says these are items you need. I must go out this morning."

Of course. I forgot I told him yesterday that I needed some things but had no time. He promised to handle it, so I suppose this is it. I recheck the email as I only skimmed it to check for Claude's approval, and sure enough it lists the specific items I need.

Sighing, I shrug and hand the paper back to her. "Yes, you're right. Thank you, Francine." I grab the credit card for her and hand it over.

"*Merci*, Jane dear." Francine practically skips to her desk and locks her computer screen before leaving the office with barely a wave at me.

Shaking my head, I set myself up and start work. I never used to trust Blake with finances as he'd spend beyond his means on things he didn't need, even had multiple credit cards to his name that he couldn't afford. We'd keep our money separate but contribute to the essential bills. That memory would explain why I'm so paranoid now.

Then why can't I shake the niggle that something isn't right?

Chapter 16

Jane

A t the end of the day, Francine comes up to my desk and places the credit card and receipts next to my arm. "Thanks, Francine."

The training session went well, I had everything I needed, so it put my worries to rest.

Francine nods and returns to her desk.

It ticks over to 4:55 p.m., so I finish what I'm doing and save my work. When I remove my bag from the drawer, I remember the gift Francine gave me earlier. Taking it out, I go over to her desk and set it next to her.

"I can't accept it. I'm sorry. I appreciate the gesture, but it's too much. You don't have to buy an apology. The coffee was enough."

Francine's mouth opens and closes a few times, but she says nothing. Instead, she nods once and pushes the box to the side. Has no one offered her friendship before? Hell, is that what I'm doing? I didn't think I wanted to be friends, but as the day has worn on, I remembered my time in high school and the struggles I had trying to fit in.

While this is a far cry from high school, Francine reminds me of me when I was the unpopular teenager trying to make friends. Yeah, she's made her mistakes and must live with the repercussions, but I don't need to make things worse.

"How would you like to meet for coffee tomorrow morning?" I ask.

Francine nods but says nothing, so I turn and go back to my desk.

"Jane," Claude comes over to me, a satchel over his shoulder, "I need you to organise some hardware purchases for new staff coming on in a couple of months. Can you do that by the end of the week?"

I keep my smile neutral. "Of course, just let me know what you need."

Is it wrong that I feel so...sidelined? Unimportant? A contract always ends, I understand that, but I've stupidly gone and grown attached to my life here. With Claude and Penny, and now Jacques, I wish I could stay. So Claude making plans that don't include me stings like hell.

Still, I've got a job to finish, and I'm going to do it well.

"Already done," Claude interrupts my thoughts, "there's an email in your inbox. I must run, but Penny wants to meet again soon."

"Sounds good. I'll message her and we'll come up with a plan."

Claude nods, waves, and speeds off.

I shake my shoulders to ease the tension and turn back to my desk to shut down my computer.

"Jane dear," Francine calls from her desk.

I turn to find her peering over the pod wall.

"I apologise for being so brash...with the necklace. I appreciate your honesty, and I am sorry if I made you uncomfortable."

Two apologies in two sentences, *three* apologies in two days. This is a record for Francine.

"It's fine, really."

"I would like to meet for coffee tomorrow, as you suggest." Francine sits back down again.

My computer powers off the same moment Jacques exits his office. He winks at me as he passes and leaves through the front door. I take this as code for "meet you outside," especially after Claude's warning yesterday.

I pick up my bag and on the way to the door stop at Francine's desk. "Are you okay to lock up?" I slip the strap of my handbag over my shoulder.

"Yes, you go. See you tomorrow morning. Same time for coffee?"

"Sounds good. *Bonsoir*, Francine."

I take my coat, gloves, and scarf off the rack, then step outside to where Jacques is waiting. The temperature has risen, and the sun is out, now lowering in the sky. The snow has melted, but it was nice while it lasted.

"Let's go." I take Jacques' hand with my free one and kiss him. "Are you still cooking tonight."

Jacques squeezes my hand as we walk off. "*Oui*, be prepared for a feast."

A

nd a feast it was. My gosh, Jacques can cook. He should be a chef, not a businessman. When I told him this, he only laughed and said he'd never considered it. Shame.

It's been two weeks since and he's cooked for me most nights. When he hasn't, he's taken me out to see more of Paris. I'm finally seeing why Paris is the city of love, and Regina was right. I do love it here...now, at least. I can thank Jacques for that, and Claude and Penny before him.

The best part of the last two weeks? The fact that Jacques and I have spent every night together. We're practically living together without moving in. We've both got things in each other's apartments. Toothpaste, toothbrushes, shower things. The only items missing are clothes. Oddly enough, each morning we change into the previous day's clothes, then go home and change before work. Inconvenient, yes, but for some reason it's stuck.

Have you ever experienced that moment when everything is *perfect*? Where you can't imagine life getting any better and *nothing* can change it?

Yeah, that's where I'm at right now. Total and utter bliss. I've been so giddily happy, even the prospect of going home isn't ruining it. I'm confident everything will be fine. The feelings between Jacques and me, the intensity of our lovemaking, is proof of that. We just need to figure out how.

Spending so much time together means we've got to know each other well, and I'm hooked. I don't want to leave Paris with a shattered heart; we need to have *the* talk. Discuss the future and how we're going to work. I have some ideas I want to run by him.

When my alarm sounds on a Wednesday morning, I sleepily decide to bring this up with him tonight. We're going out again; he's taking me to the restaurant at the Eiffel Tower. We're meeting Penny and Claude, too, so I'm super excited.

I snake my arm out of the warmth of Jacques' bed to snooze the alarm, then settle back down, pulling the covers up to my chin.

The bed moves as Jacques rolls over to drag me into his warmth and whisper his usual, "*Bonjour beauté*," in my ear. A quick kiss on my shoulder then he gets out of bed. No snooze for Jacques, I've learned. As soon as the alarm goes off, he's out of bed.

The nights at Jacques' place are definitely the best. Although interestingly, we tend to spend more nights at mine than at his. I get the feeling he likes my small, albeit cosy, apartment, even if he's never said so.

I doze lightly, vaguely aware of the shower running in the background. When the snooze goes off, I set it one last time and wake fully when the second one goes off. Pushing the covers back, I sit up and reach for the white t-shirt Jacques loaned me last night, donning it. It's too big for me, but it's perfect for relaxing in.

I go into the bathroom to use the toilet, then after washing my hands, I go out through the second door into the living area. I expect to see Jacques in the kitchen preparing coffee, but instead he's cornered by a well-dressed couple. His parents.

All three turn to me when I exit, and I halt, my face turning red hot. Hyper aware I'm in nothing but a t-shirt, I tug on the hem and manage an awkward smile.

"Uh, hi." My forced smile feels like a cringe.

Last time I saw Jacques' mother, she was rugged up yet still elegant. Today without the layers her elegance is out of this world. Geez. Francine, eat your heart out.

Perfectly styled honey-brown hair, perfect makeup, a fashionable dusty pink pantsuit with a white silk blouse, white heels, and loads of gold jewellery. She dresses to impress and is not afraid to show she's from money. She turns to me, her straight, pointed nose stuck in the air.

Seems they have a habit of turning up early. At least today it's later; it's just gone seven thirty a.m. I don't remember hearing the intercom buzz, though. Must've gone off while I was snoozing.

Jacques sends me an apologetic look and blusters a little before saying, "Maman, Papa, this is Jane. She is my girlfriend."

A little thrill traipses down my spine, and I would've grinned like a fool if I wasn't in the second most awkward situation of my life. My first involved a high school crush and me chasing him for a kiss. That is *not* a story I wish to retell. Ever.

"Jane, this is Angélique and Marcel DuPont, my parents," Jacques says.

"*This* is your girlfriend?" Angélique's voice is soft, almost regal. The way she says it confirms she knew I existed.

Her English is impeccable, too, although this doesn't surprise me. Everything else about her is so perfect.

"*Oui*, Maman," Jacques responds.

Angélique eyes me critically from head to toe, clearly not impressed, before sniffing and turning to Jacques. "*She* is the reason you left the family company?"

"*Non*, Maman," Jacques sounds exasperated, "I left by choice. Jane only encourages me to do what I wish to do."

"She does, does she?" Angélique narrows her eyes.

Marcel takes Jacques' attention, handing him a leather folder, and they start talking. As Jacques opens it, his face pales. I'm tempted to go over and eavesdrop, but Angélique is moving toward me, ever so gracefully, like she's floating.

I tug on the t-shirt, hoping to stretch it, to no avail. Angélique stops in front of me, tall and regal-like, with a swan-like neck and flawless skin. A waft of delicate, flowery perfume catches my nose. Agonisingly slowly, she rakes her gaze over me from head to toe, her nose wrinkling in...is that disgust?

I swallow hard, but my heat is racing, and all I want to do is run back into Jacques' room and hide. If I'd heard them arrive, I would have.

"You might have the long legs and the blond hair and the pretty blue eyes, but you will never be good enough for Jacques." She's talking quietly, but her tone is venomous, her words hitting like daggers. "Have your bit of fun, but you will never be welcome in our family. Jacques will always be a DuPont, and he has a duty to his name."

Holy hell, this woman is *insane.* I can't look away from her piercing hazel gaze, so hard, so cool, so calm.

"You don't even know me," I say, annoyed that the tremble in my voice makes me sound weak.

She smirks and shakes her head. "I do not need to. You are not French. That is all I need to know."

Her words hurt and tears sting my eyes. I blink rapidly to stop them from falling. I shouldn't let her get to me. Jacques warned me his family weren't nice, but I hadn't expected such a personal attack.

Angélique holds her head high, then turns and glides out of the apartment, leaving behind an air of perfume and throwing something in French to Marcel over her shoulder.

Marcel glances at me with a similar distaste to Angélique but otherwise doesn't acknowledge me. Jacques looks concerned, but Marcel takes his attention yet again, and they start bickering in French.

Overwhelmed, I back into the bathroom and close the door, leaning against it. I'm breathing heavily and my heart is racing, but I manage to control my tears. This isn't going to be a one-off. If I really want a relationship with Jacques, I need to deal with it.

We've been lucky these last two weeks as he's had no contact with family, and we've been in our little bubble. Even the divide I'd noticed between Jacques and me had closed. I finally felt like I belonged.

Now this.

Maybe I was right to worry after all.

Chapter 17

Jacques

"What will you do if your business fails?" Papa asks in French, his dark, serious eyes trained on me. "You will lose everything. Once you are out of this will," he points to the leather folder in my hand, "I will not revise it again. And I will not make another business proposition, either."

"I will not fail." I pull my shoulders back.

It is the first time I see genuine concern in Papa's eyes. "You cannot be sure of that. Running a business is hard work. Jacques," he sighs and rests a hand on my shoulder, squeezing hard, "do you care about that woman in there?" He nods in the direction of the bathroom Jane disappeared into a few minutes ago.

My heart skips, and I nod without hesitation. "Yes, Papa. I know you and Maman do not approve, but it is not up to either of you to decide who I date."

"No, you are right." His gaze hardens. "But when your business fails—"

My nostrils flare as I step back, Papa's hand slipping off my shoulder. "It will *not* fail! I can run a business, Papa. In that area you taught me well."

That is the *only* area. I am tempted to list the other areas he failed, but it will not be wise. We have been bickering since his arrival, and I am fed up. Fuelling the fire will only draw it out when I want him gone so I can spend the morning with Jane.

Papa shrugs in defeat and steps back toward the door. "I hope for your sake that you are right." He opens the door but turns back to add, "Because I guarantee she is only interested in your money, and when it runs out, she *will* leave you."

He leaves, the door closing after him.

I drop the leather folder on the kitchen island. "*Merde!*"

Is he right? Am I doomed to fail without Entreprises DuPont beside my name? I was born and bred into this life, and the company is all that I have ever known. It seems, though, that I am the only one who can see beneath the surface to the shady dealings below. The unsatisfied clients. The lawsuits. The mistreatment of staff.

Whether he is right or not, I cannot in my right mind continue to work for someone like that. Still, Papa's words wreak havoc in my mind. Jane never showed any interest in my money. She only ever encouraged me to be frugal.

But what if Papa is right? What if she has put on an act but she really is like all the others? The ones who have only been interested in status and money. There is a reason I am still single. I have not yet found that one person who accepts me for me. I thought Jane was it.

Mon Dieu, Papa has got into my head, and I need him out. I do not like the doubt creeping in.

A hand on my back makes me jump, and Jane appears at my side.

"Sorry," she smiles apologetically, "I didn't mean to scare you. Is everything okay? With your parents?"

Instinct is to plaster on a smile and nod. "*Oui*," I push away from the island, kiss her swiftly, then go around and turn on the coffee machine, "he only came by to remind me that I have until the end of the day to change my mind."

I can sense Jane's gaze on me, following my every move as I move from the coffee machine to the fridge, removing eggs, butter, and chives to make a French omelette.

"Are *you* okay?" Jane asks softly.

"I am good." I take the salt out of a cupboard and turn to flash her my best convincing smile. I am unsure if I succeed, but I cannot let her in on my thoughts. The last thing I want to do is hurt her.

She sighs but does not push the subject, of which I am thankful.

I start on the first coffee as Jane's arms wrap around my waist. While it is filtering, I spin around and smile into Jane's beautiful blue eyes. She is still wearing my white t-shirt, which only just covers her derrière, and is very sexy.

"Coffee?" I ask.

"*Oui, s'il vous plait*," she says with a cheeky grin.

I hold a hand over my heart and groan dramatically. "You speak the language better, but your accent is terrible." I roll my eyes. "I will keep teaching you."

Over the last two weeks, we have both been helping each other. I am helping her improve her French, and she is helping me with my English. We do not misunderstand each other as much, but we still have a long way to go.

"Go on," she breathes, winding her arms around my neck, "teach me."

Coffee and food forgotten, I waste no time kissing her thoroughly. She is an exceptional kisser, and I hope to enjoy these moments forever. I pick Jane up effortlessly, and she wraps her legs around my waist. I stumble over to the sofa and gently lower her onto its softness. Pulling apart for air, we both draw in large breaths as we stare at each other for a long, long moment.

A smile blossoms on Jane's face when she whispers in perfect French, "*Je t'aime*, Jacques DuPont," then she pulls my head down to meet her lips for another kiss.

Unexpected tears prick my eyes. Her words wash over me and seep into my soul, stirring my deepest emotions. Words I did not realise I needed to hear, yet now want to hear every day. She is *mon amour*, and I want to spend the rest of my life with her.

The words are on the tip of my tongue. I desperately want to say them back because I do love her. I am *in* love with her. But—

Papa's words flood back into my mind, and I pull away with a gasp. Sitting back, I rake a hand through my hair. This cannot go on. His words will continue to taunt me, and I will only be able to silence them by putting my mind at ease.

Jane sits up, her face ashen. "Jack, I'm so sorry, I shouldn't have—"

I shake my head, and the words spew out before I can stop myself. "Why are you with me, Jane?"

Her eyes widen, and she tugs at her t-shirt. "What? I just told you I loved you." Her face turns red, and she turns away, blinking rapidly. "Isn't that enough?"

I feel like a *bâtard*, but I cannot rest easy until I clear Papa's words from my mind. "What happens if my business fails?"

"Not all businesses succeed. If it fails, well, you learn from it and try again." She turns back to me, and my breath catches. Her eyes are shining with unshed tears. "I don't understand why you're asking this."

I sigh and rest my elbows on my legs, placing my head in my hands. "If my business fails, I could lose everything. And if I am removed from the family will—"

"Oh, I get it," she sneers. When I look back up at her, I see the realisation on her face. "Let me guess, your father said I'm only interested in your money." She scoffs and stands from the sofa, pacing the floor.

I nod and lower my head in shame. I should not have let his words get to me, but once they were in my head, they would not leave.

"And you *believed* him?"

"No...I do not know." I groan and scrub my hands over my face. "I do not want to believe him, but every other—" I snap my mouth closed before the words can come out, but it is too late.

The hurt on Jane's face cuts me to the core. "Have I ever behaved like these other women who were only interested in your money and status?"

I look at her in silent apology and shake my head. She is the most real woman I ever met, and I hate that Papa made me doubt her.

"I don't come from money," she continues. "I'm used to living hand to mouth. Sure, I'm all for improving my financial status, but I don't need luxurious things, and I'm not going to get involved with you *just* for your money. I'm okay with a simple life." She comes over and kneels in front of me, looking me square in the eyes. "The big question is, are you? I think that's the biggest issue here. Are *you* ready for a different life in the off-chance that your business fails?"

I never thought of it like that before. I cannot comprehend life without money, which is why breaking away from the family company is so terrifying. And Papa knows this; it is why he planted doubt in my mind.

I am silent too long.

Jane sighs. "You think money is all you need for a happy life." She gets to her feet. "I love you for *you*, Jack, not for your bank account. I was a fool to want the same in return." She turns and goes into my bedroom.

For a moment I remain motionless, her words hanging in the air. I am stunned. She has that little faith in me...in *us*?

"You are wrong." I follow her into the bedroom and stop inside the doorway. "I know having a happy life involves more than having money. You taught me that." She is changing, but she does not look at me. "Do you really think I care about your bank account?"

I wait for her to speak, but she still says nothing, only sits on the bed to put her shoes on. Cold fear is raging through my veins. Fear that I am not enough for her. Fear that she thinks our lives are so different, and she is too scared to commit to me.

"I do not care about any of that." I sit on the bed beside her. "Jane, please look at me."

She slips on her last shoe and finally looks at me, her eyes brimming with tears.

"Papa got into my head and I doubted you. For that, I am sorry. You need to believe that I trust you, Jane, wholly and completely, and

I *do not* care about your monetary or social status in life." I reach for her hand and entwine our fingers. "There is one area in which you are right, though."

Two tears slide down her cheeks, but there is hope in her eyes, and this spurs me on. This is my final chance.

"You are right in that comprehending life without money is not easy for me. But if it comes to that, I can do it with you by my side. With you, anything is possible because you help me see beyond my privilege. *I only need you.*" I hold her gaze and emphasise those last words, *needing* her to hear me. To believe me.

I swear the hope in her eyes grows. A small smile kicks up at the corners of her lips, but then a shutter comes down and the hope is gone. What has caused it?

Her shoulders slacken, and she shakes her head. "No, Jack, you're wrong. I've come into your life at the wrong time. You're at this new juncture, breaking away from your family and your privileged life. You've got a lot to figure out, I get it. But how can we even think about a relationship? About how *we're* going to survive with all this as well?"

This is not making sense. I do not understand. "Jane, please do not—"

She squeezes my hand. "Please don't stop me, Jack. You know I'm right. This is a huge transition for you, and you need to come to terms with your new life. Figure out what *you* want. Get away from your family and stand on your own two feet. On your own."

"No, you are wrong!" My heart is heavy in my chest. "Why can we not travel this path together? I believe we are strong enough."

She does not answer. Instead, she removes her hand from mine and stands, starting for the door.

"Am I not good enough for you?" I ask after her. "Is that what this is about?"

Jane stops and shakes her head. "That's not it at all, Jack. You're *too* good."

What is that supposed to mean? I am at a loss and do not know what to say. A thousand words are going around my head, a mixture of English and French, and I am struggling to choose which ones to use. I want to speak French because it is easier, but she will not understand me very well.

Jane leaves the room, and I leap up off the bed, following her. "I love you, Jane," I say in the best English I can manage.

She stumbles to a stop and turns back to me. "Jack, please don't—"

I stride up to her and stop, wrapping one arm around her waist and using my free hand to stroke her cheek. She looks up at me. Her face is red. Her eyes are brimming with tears, her cheeks wet with the ones she already wept.

"I love you," I repeat. "Please do not leave."

I capture her lips and pour every ounce of emotion into it. My love for her. My frustration at the situation. My anger at Papa's interference. Mingled with her tears, and even a couple of my own, it is the sweetest, most heartbreaking kiss of my life.

"I'm sorry, Jack," Jane whispers when we pull apart, then she writhes out of my grasp and runs out of my apartment. And my life.

Chapter 18

Jane

That test? Yeah, it broke us. Or did *I* break us?

Oh, crap.

I totally freaked out back there. First there was Angélique telling me I'm not good enough. Then Jacques doubted me. Sure, he apologised, but if anything's gonna scare a girl away, that will do it. If I'm honest, Angélique takes the cake. And suddenly the divide between us was just too wide to jump over.

How can I deny the truth of her words? I'm a fool to think Jacques and I had a chance. I've always known we were worlds apart, and she only proved my point. Whether I like it or not, this is for the best.

I'm in a total daze as I rush home, shower, change, and rush out again, trying my hardest not to think about what I just did to Jacques. I did the right thing.

I *did.*

I arrive at Café de Paris and stop outside to gather my bearings. I draw in a long breath and release it slowly. Today is the first day I haven't needed a jacket. I'm even wearing a skirt and a short-sleeve blouse. The weather has turned, and the cold is gone. The morning is surprisingly warm, just how I like it, but I can't enjoy it. Not when my heart is in pieces.

It doesn't help that our last kiss is replaying in my mind like a movie reel. I felt every single one of Jacques emotions. His love. His frustration. His anger. His heartbreak at what I did to him...to us. For someone who's struggled with showing emotion, he certainly knew how to show it in a kiss.

It will live with me forever. I think I'm going to become a spinster and be that crazy cat lady with dozens of cats. Did I tell you I love cats?

Gritting my teeth, I go inside.

"*Puis-je vous aider?*" The barista is asking if he can help me.

I force a smile and step forward, placing my usual cappuccino order. Thankfully I'm *not* meeting Francine this morning. I don't think I can handle her today.

As I step back to wait, I don't feel like myself. It's like I'm on the outside looking in. I'm here, but also not. The next four weeks feel like an eternity now. How the hell are Jacques and I supposed to work together?

It's a good thing I'm a pro at avoiding people I don't want to face.

When my coffee is ready, I'm not really thinking, and I grab it by the lid. I realise too late the lid is loose and the cup falls out, landing on the floor. I gasp as hot coffee splashes up my bare legs, seeps into my shoes, and forms a puddle on the floor around my feet.

"*Je suis vraiment désolé,*" I clumsily manage an apology as another barista rushes out with a mop and bucket. I grab a handful of serviettes and crouch to start cleaning up, but I'm shooed away.

"*J'ai ça.*" She smiles kindly, telling me she's got this.

I'm not entirely sure why she's being so kind when I flooded the café with coffee. But as I stand, the door opens and a breeze wafts in, cool on my face, and I realise with horror that I'm crying. Over a bloody cappuccino. I'm literally crying over spilt milk.

Can my day possibly get any worse?

"*Merci,*" I say with a wobbly smile, wiping my tears away with the serviettes and using the rest to wipe my legs dry.

Finding a bin close by, I dump the serviettes when I hear from the counter, "*Excusez-moi!*"

I glance across to the other barista who has made another cappuccino for me. "*Celui-ci est sur nous.*" He says the coffee is on them.

It takes every ounce of effort to hold back my tears as I approach him and pick it up with the best smile I can muster. This time by the actual cup and *not* the lid.

Unable to speak, I send one last smile before dashing out of the café, my feet squelching in my soggy shoes. I hide at the side of the building to pull myself together. My chest feels like it's going to burst open as the tears cascade down my cheeks. The pain of everything that's happened today is coming out in hacking sobs. How am I supposed to work with Jacques there? But I can't *not* work, either.

Removing a packet of tissues from my bag, I take a few deep breaths and wipe my tears away. After a few sips of my coffee, I start to calm down.

I can do this. *I can.*

Despite the emotions wreaking havoc inside me, I make my way to work and slip into the office without any fanfare. After dropping my bag and coffee at my desk, I make a detour to the bathroom. When my feet are clean and my shoes are semi-dry, I go back and settle down to work.

Francine pokes her head above the partition and sends me a sickly sweet smile. "*Bonjour*, Jane dear."

I tried so hard to be friendly and patient with her. We have coffee twice a week, but nothing melts the ice constantly surrounding her.

Maybe it's just her, but I'm done trying.

With my emotions in check at last, I finally begin to feel calm, and I manage to send her a polite smile.

Then Claude walks in.

I smile and lift my hand in a wave, but his icy gaze lands on me, and I shiver. Oh no, has Jacques told him already?

"My office, now," he says in a low voice before storming to his office.

If he's upset, I understand. He and Jacques are mates. But to be *that* angry?

On trembling legs, I stand and make the walk of shame to his office. Claude didn't make a scene about wanting to see me, but I'm certain everyone is looking at me. When I reach his door and look back, no one is. It's all in my mind. Well, Francine is, but she doesn't count. She watches everything I do.

Taking a deep breath, I run my sweaty hands along my skirt, then enter Claude's office. Butterflies are doing loop the loop in my stomach, making me nauseous.

When I step inside, closing the door behind me, the atmosphere is frigid, and not because of the air conditioning. There *is* no air conditioning.

Shivering, I look at Claude, whose face is dark and he won't even make eye contact. My legs nearly give way. I stumble and grab a nearby chair.

"What's going on?" I choke out, my voice not sounding like my own.

"Please sit down, Jane." Claude gestures to the chair I'm holding.

He's in professional mode, all business-like and managerial. Not good. Pulling the chair out, I sit, or rather I *fall* into it. My heart is racing, but I have no idea what's going on.

"Can you explain this?" Claude hands over a wad of paper.

Frowning, I take it from him and scan the first page. It's a credit card statement from a bank. At first the list of transactions is nothing out of the ordinary. General business expenses, all of which I provided receipts for. Even the coffee from when Jacques first started.

But then I get further down, starting from about two weeks ago. Turning to the next page, my stomach drops to my toes when I see the bright pink and yellow highlight over a bunch of purchases. The pink highlighted ones are the supplies Claude had supposedly approved Francine to buy.

"Can you explain these?" Claude's gaze meets mine in challenge. "The accounts team tells me all the purchases were not pre-approved. The pink highlight is where receipts were provided, but otherwise they received no receipts, and they don't appear to be business related."

Not pre-approved. His words run around in my head. I try to swallow, but my throat is like sandpaper. "I didn't make these purchases."

"But they were against your credit card." Claude's voice is even, but I can hear the doubt.

"I can see that, but the purchases highlighted in pink were the two separate ones you approved Francine to buy."

Claude starts and sits straighter in his chair. "I what? I never approved Francine to purchase anything."

The room begins to spin, and nausea washes over me in a cold wave. I sigh and close my eyes.

"Are you okay?" Claude asks. "Do you need water?"

I shake my head and open my eyes. The spinning stops, but the nausea lingers. "Francine had an email from you both times. They had the items listed that you needed her to buy, and you'd approved for her to use my credit card."

"Right, so I approved multiple clothes purchases, did I?" Claude snatches the statement from me and scans it. "I also apparently approved shoes totalling two hundred euros. A *three-hundred-euro* expense at a jeweller." He throws the statement down and glares at me, a vein twitching in his neck.

"O-obviously you didn't approve those ones," I stammer, sweat beading on my forehead. "They weren't on the lists, but the pink highlighted ones were." I clear my throat and avert my gaze when I add, "I can't explain the yellow highlight."

I wince and close my eyes again to hold back threatening tears. Why didn't I triple check the first purchase with Claude? I *knew* he was too distracted, but then Jacques came along, and I forgot everything else. As for the second one, I shouldn't have assumed Claude chose Francine to do the shopping.

The only thing that makes any logical sense is that she must've overheard me talking to Claude the day before. It would've been easy enough for her to intercept the person he asked to make the purchases and tell a believable lie so she could do it instead.

This is a nightmare.

Claude sighs. When I look at him, I can tell he's torn. He wants to believe me, but he must consider the whole situation.

"Remember one night a couple of weeks ago?" I ask. "I asked you if you approved Francine to buy some office supplies?"

Claude's expression is blank. "You did?"

I slump in my chair.

"I'm sorry," Claude sounds genuinely apologetic, "I must've misunderstood or misheard the question."

"You were distracted." My voice is harder than I intend it to be.

"Hey, don't turn this into my fault." Claude holds his hands up. "I'm sorry I don't remember, but you could have asked again."

I wince and nod. "I know, but Claude, you must trust me."

He looks at me long and hard, nodding. "I do, but that doesn't make everything all right. Unless you can provide proof of your accusations, this is on *your* head. I can overlook the receipted purchases, but the yellow," he shakes his head, "it's fraud, Jane."

My heart leaps and I turn cold. Fraud? Good lord, he's right.

"Can you prove anything?" he asks. "Do you have copies of those emails?"

I bite my lip and lower my gaze, shaking my head. "On both occasions, she handed me a printed copy of the email, and I gave it back. It was instinctive." I'm such an idiot. There was always a niggle of doubt in the back of my mind, but I let my guard down because I thought I was doing the right thing.

She claims to know nothing about computers, always asking for my help, yet she can create fake emails? Oh no, she knew *exactly* what she was doing, and I didn't give her enough bitch credits for her attempts, and succeeding, at manipulation.

She's set me up, got me right where she wants me. Out of here. Because there's no way I'm continuing with this job for another four weeks. No way in hell.

Everything becomes clear now. The necklace, the new clothes, new shoes, which I missed. She even waited two weeks before wearing them! The conniving bitch used the company credit card and set out to blame me. And clearly, she's been planning for a while. When she couldn't access my desk, she did the next best thing. And succeeded.

All because she doesn't like me. Or more specifically, doesn't like the changes being made to the company, and I was put there to implement some of them. I wonder if she knew about me and Jacques, too. If she'd started eavesdropping on my conversations, she probably did. And if so, she might've been jealous. Not of *us*, but of him taking her job so she went through me as the "easy target."

"Are you certain you didn't send the emails and approve the purchases?" I ask desperately, looking back up at him. "If you've got them in your sent box—"

"I'm one hundred percent certain, and if you want to look for yourself, that's fine. But I would *never* trust Francine with something like this." His brow furrows in confusion. "I'm surprised you did."

I throw my hands up. "You'd already spoken to me about my behaviour toward Francine, told me to make more of an effort. I figured if you trusted her, then I could. The emails were extremely realistic and easy to fake. If she had even one email from you, copy and paste, rewrite, print, done."

Ugh, I shouldn't know this.

Claude winces. "I understand, Jane, but it doesn't solve the problem. We've got hundreds of euros in purchases that are unaccounted for and unauthorised." He rubs his temples and sighs. "I'm going to talk to Francine, too, but if she denies everything and there is no proof—" His gaze is apologetic. "Without evidence, there won't be any legal proceedings, but there is no three-strike rule in this case. Fraud is immediate dismissal, and you will have to go home."

Tears threaten to fall, and I nod mechanically.

It's official, my day *can* get worse.

But after what happened with Jacques, this isn't such a terrible fate. I want to go home. To my friends and family. To somewhere I'm wanted, needed, and *liked*.

⁓⚬⚬⁓

F rancine denied everything.

Not that I'm surprised. She's not stupid enough to admit to it after she went to all the trouble to set me up. Only *I'm* the stupid one here. I should've kept the emails, or at least copied them, locked them away, *anything*. But now she gets to keep her job and my life in Paris is over. Shows what happens when you try to be friends with a bitch.

Claude is nice enough to let me stay the whole the day, so I don't have to do the shameful pack-up-desk-and-leave in the middle of the day. At five p.m., when it's only me, Francine, and Claude in his office, I start packing up. I glance at Jacques' office, I can't help myself, and the seed of worry grows in my gut. He hasn't been in all day. Claude hasn't said anything about what happened, so I assume he doesn't know.

Shaking my head, I push the thoughts away. I don't want to think about it. About him. Because I'm afraid I might've made a massive mistake. If I did, I can't fix it. Not after this disaster at work.

After emailing Claude important documents and a rundown of what else needs to be done, I delete everything off my hard drive. I log off, pack up my belongings in my handbag, then stand, taking one last look around. I'm not ready for this, not so soon.

Claude pokes his head out of the office, gives me a sad, apologetic smile and a wave before going back in. I'm thankful he trusts me enough to see myself out rather than acting like a security guard. That would've been embarrassing. I want to ask him why he can trust me now but not when it comes to the credit card fraud, but I don't.

I understand it, I really do; I'm just bitter.

Slipping the strap of my handbag over my shoulder, I make my way to the door, passing Francine's desk. As I do, she chirps, "*Au revoir*, Jane."

My intention is to walk straight past. Don't provoke her. But since I've lost my job, I figure I have nothing to lose. I think I have the right to tell Francine what I think.

I stop and turn to her with what I hope is an expressionless face. The moment I see her smug "I win" grin, anger boils low in my belly. She is *not* getting away with this completely. She might get to keep the job, but I've got the clear conscience. Yeah, I made a mistake, but it was unintentional.

"*Tu es une chienne*, Francine," I call her a bitch in my best French ever. Well, apart from telling Jacques I love him.

My heart skips at the reminder of leaving him behind. Seriously, now is *not* the time to be thinking about this.

Her shocked expression is *so* worth it, and I'm able to push my thoughts aside. I'm not done yet. Glancing back over my shoulder to make sure Claude isn't watching, I step closer to Francine's desk and hiss, "You're a spineless, arrogant, *horrible* woman, and I hope you rot in hell. You lied to Claude today, and you know it."

She quickly recovers, but I don't miss the fear in her eyes. She pulls her shoulders back and sticks her nose in the air. "I do not know what you are talking about." She turns away with a sniff.

"Yes, you do, and I hope the guilt eats away at you forever. Just remember, karma is a bitch, and every time it touches you, you're going to remember me and what you did. I'm very glad I'll never work with you again."

With a final sweet smile her way, I turn and leave the office.

If I learned anything from my time at Maître Tech, it's that I can't let people like Francine, and Blake, walk all over me. If I have a bad feeling about something, or someone, I'm going to listen to it. I will speak up rather than deal with it alone. I've spent too many years doing that, and today it stops.

Chapter 19

Jane

Numb. That's what I am. Completely numb.

My logical brain kept me going today, getting things done that I need to do.

Contact immigration. Check. I have forty-eight hours to sort my life out and leave the country.

Book a return flight. Check. I leave tomorrow afternoon. Take that, immigration! I know how to work quickly.

Return to my apartment, collapse on the floor, and sob for hours. Check, check, and check.

Many hours later, after giving myself a stern talking to, I pull myself together. My apartment is in darkness apart from a sliver of light coming through the gap in my curtains. Getting to my feet, my body protests from sitting in one position for too long.

I'm not a wallower; I never have been. Until today when my whole world turned upside down. But now it stops. Move on. No more crying.

I've got this.

I've still got to break the news to everyone in Australia. If the many attempts to phone me is anything to go by, Regina already knows. I haven't answered because I wasn't ready to face reality. I'll call her later. She deserves the truth, and she needs to decide if *she's* going to let me keep my job in Australia, too…

Ugh.

Turning on the lamp on my bedside cupboard, I wince at the brightness. When my eyes adjust, I check my phone for the time. Seven p.m. There are also four missed calls and five messages from Penny.

Bugger, I forgot we were supposed to be meeting for dinner tonight at the Eiffel Tower. I never got around to cancelling with her. What does she know? Anything?

Claude should've told her about what happened at work, but I have no idea if Jacques told them anything.

I unlock my phone and wince when I read Penny's messages, each one escalating in panic as more time passes.

Her first one comes through at six p.m.

I know what happened at work today. Claude told me. That doesn't mean you get out of dinner. Claude is on babysitting duties. You and I are still meeting. Jacques is welcome too. See you at 6:30.

So she knows about my job but not about Jacques. Well, that's just dandy.

Her next message is five minutes before six thirty p.m.

I'm here and you're not. I'm giving you the benefit of the doubt that you're still on your way.

One call comes in fifteen minutes later, then a message five minutes after that.

Jane, this isn't funny. Are you coming or not? I'm getting worried.

Another call ten minutes later and another message.

Jane, please tell me you're okay? I know this must be hard on you, but please don't shut me out.

Five minutes later, there are three more calls within minutes, and one last message that came through a minute ago.

If you don't contact me in the next five minutes, I'm calling the police.

Feeling bad for worrying her, I send her a quick reply.

I'm okay. I'll be there in half an hour. Wait for me.

The last thing I feel like doing is going to the Eiffel Tower. Too many memories. Too much hurt. But if I have to go home, I can't leave without saying goodbye to Penny.

I'm out of my apartment in five minutes flat and running to the metro. Despite how stuffy, crowded, and smelly it is, I realise I'm going to miss it when I return to Australia. In fact, I'm going to miss a lot about Paris.

A train screeches into the station, and I shuffle on board with a hoard of people, everyone pushing and shoving to get inside before the doors close again.

Everything feels so final, making my heart heavier and heavier. Yes, I'm looking forward to seeing my friends and family, but I still don't want to leave. Without Jacques, nothing makes sense anymore. I knew where I wanted to be and what I wanted. Without a doubt, *we* could work.

Who says we couldn't swap countries? Six months in Australia, six months in France. But we never got to have that discussion. Now it's too late.

Tears threaten to fall again, but I sniff and blink them away. No more tears, remember? Besides, I don't want to be that crazy lady crying on the train.

I note the stop we're at and move closer to the door so I can get off at the next one. Moments later, I arrive at the Eiffel Tower, panting from running. I stop a few feet away and gawp up at the huge tower. Up close, it's even more impressive and bright.

I'm reminded of Jacques again and our first official "date," even if it was a setup. The best setup ever. I draw in a shuddering breath at the memory.

It's still so crazy how quickly we clicked after we talked and spent some time together. We were from two different worlds, but we were both lonely in Paris. I was lonely because I didn't fit in. He was lonely because only Penny and Claude saw him as a real human. Everyone else only ever saw his name and status. We were both lost in this vast world, trying to find our feet.

Then we found each other, connected on a level I think neither of us expected, and the world made sense again. We helped each other, and it wasn't so overwhelming anymore. He helped me fit in, helped me improve my French, and showed me the beauty of Paris. I helped him...how? Sure, I tried to be supportive and encouraged him to embrace his new life. But what did I do to help him achieve it?

Told him that he had to do this on his own.

Holy cow. What was I *thinking*? Am I totally heartless? *Am I Francine?*

"Jane!" Penny's voice calls over the hubbub of people lining up to get into the tower. "Jane, over here!"

I spot Penny at the entrance, waving with both arms. Paralysed, I'm torn between meeting Penny and running to Jacques' apartment to apologise. My insides are jumping about, my feet are urging me to leave, but after Penny's near meltdown, I can't leave her, either.

With a shake of my head, I go over to her. There is no missing the dirty glances as I skip the queue.

"Thank God you're here." Penny embraces me. She lets me go and grasps my hand, trying to pull me inside. I remain rooted to the spot.

"Jane," she huffs in frustration, "these tables are hard to get. I only *just* managed to convince the waiter to let me wait this long."

"Jacques and I broke up," I blurt. Just speaking the words is painful, and I'm so angry at myself for giving up so easily.

"You *what?*" Penny shrieks.

"I did a really stupid thing." My heart is racing, and my breath is coming out in short bursts. I grip my head and shake it, struggling to find the words. "I-I don't know what to do." I look around frantically, but it doesn't help.

"Jane," Penny loops her arm through mine, and I turn to her, "let's sit down, have something to eat, and you can tell me everything. You're practically shaking. You need to stop, breathe, and calm down."

Stop. Breathe. Calm down. Yes, good idea. I take a deep breath and release it slowly, which in turn starts to slow my racing heart. Eating might help, too, as I skipped lunch and didn't have time for breakfast. No wonder I'm so bloody emotional and confused.

"Okay," I concede.

Penny smiles and keeps her arm looped through mine as she leads me over to the elevator. The stairs are closed for the night. That's one thing I hoped to do with Jacques—climb the tower. I was going to suggest it this weekend.

My sigh gets Penny's attention. "Are you okay?" she asks as the elevator doors open.

We step in with a few other people, and Penny presses the button for the second level.

I look at her through watery eyes and shake my head but say nothing. If I do, I'm going to be a blubbering mess.

She nods but doesn't ask any more questions. The elevator doors open, and we step out into a crowded restaurant. To my relief, Penny leads me through to a dark corner at the back and lets me sit with my back to the restaurant.

We sit in silence for a few minutes, Penny giving me time to pull myself together. Now a little calmer, I realise how much I need this. Penny and me, catching up like old friends.

Once settled, my addled brain goes to the easiest thing to talk about. "I'm sorry I didn't reply to you earlier." I give Penny my best apologetic smile. "Everything happened at once today. I wasn't thinking."

Penny picks up her menu and looks at me over it. "I understand, and it's okay."

I pick up my own menu and scan it over, wincing.

"It's on me," Penny says, probably seeing me wince. "No arguments. You need this tonight."

I smile gratefully and go back to scanning, looking for the most comforting meal. The waiter comes for our orders, then once he's left, Penny folds her arms on the table and stares right at me.

"Before we talk about Jacques, I need you to know that Claude is in my bad books after what happened today and I'm on your side." She nods once, determination written across her features. "What he did today is bloody unforgivable. Seriously, thinking *you* stole from the company when Francine's had it in for you from the beginning. Pfft."

I shake my head, needing to defend Claude. A day of emotional outbursts and tons of thinking helped me realise a few harsh truths.

"I appreciate your support, Penny," I reach across to squeeze her hand, "but you forget how difficult the situation was for Claude, too. He can't blame Francine when there was no evidence whatsoever, *and* she denied everything. At the end of the day, the credit card had *my* name on the front, and I gave it to her without confirming with Claude. I was encouraged to trust her a little, and I trusted her *too* much."

Penny shakes her head, but the anger on her face lessens. "What exactly happened? Claude said he couldn't tell me, confidentiality or some rubbish."

I smile sadly, silently thanking Claude for being responsible like always, then tell her everything.

"You're too nice, Jane." Penny smiles at the waiter when he delivers our meals. "I wouldn't be so forgiving if it were me."

"I don't want to be," I pick up my fork, "but I'm partially to blame. No, it's not fair, but you know the details. I can't stay angry at Claude, but it does sting, and it might take me a while to be able to face him again."

Penny smiles in understanding but says nothing. We eat in silence for a few minutes, but the food doesn't agree with me; instead, it settles like lead in the pit of my stomach. I only make it through half the meal when nausea overcomes me, and I have to stop.

"So, about Jacques," Penny waves her fork in the air with a prawn speared on it, "you broke it off?"

I push my plate away and sigh. I feel a bit calmer, but the food hasn't helped like I hoped. Now I'm bloated *and* emotional.

I tell Penny what happened this morning, including the confrontation with Angélique.

"Oh, Jane," Penny shakes her head, "you're such an idiot."

"Excuse me?"

"You heard me. Jacques said he needed you and you walk out? He's willing to give up his *entire life* for you. Don't you think *he* can choose for himself how he wants to live it? If he chooses to be with you, even during this so-called transition you talk about, embrace it! If you lose Jacques DuPont, you'll never find anyone remotely like him, that I can promise you."

My heart is heavy with the realisation that she's right. But maybe I don't deserve Jacques DuPont.

Penny grabs my hand and holds it tight. "I get it. Angélique is a terrifying figure, I've met her myself, but she doesn't control you *or* Jacques. She tried to freak you out, and she succeeded."

I shake my head in frustration. "I know."

"What are you going to do?" Penny asks after the waiter removes our plates.

"What can I do?" I lift my hands up, then let them drop again. "Tomorrow I have to go home. Might as well draw a line in the sand and start over. You're right, I'll never meet another Jacques DuPont, but it's for the best. I would never fit into that life."

Penny stares at me, agape. "You what? You didn't tell me you had to go home tomorrow!"

I wince. "I'm sorry, we had so many other things to talk about. Immigration gave me an exemption long enough for me to gather my things and book a flight, but otherwise my hands are tied. I'm officially an illegal immigrant. Unless a sponsor for a job falls in my lap in the next twelve hours, that's that. My life here is done. My relationship with Jacques is done. It's back to my old Aussie life again."

"Are you certain leaving without talking to Jacques is the right thing to do?" Penny's gaze levels with mine.

"I'm not certain about anything," I say with a half laugh, half hiccup.

Deep down, I desperately want to see him, but I fear turning up unannounced will give him false hope. I'll send him a message later.

Or maybe I won't.

I don't know. It's probably best if I just slip away.

"I'm going to miss you, Jane, but I do have some positive news. I booked flights to Australia for December. I'll be coming with Claude and Amélie, and we *are* going to catch up whether you like it or not. Until then, we're keeping in constant contact. Zoom chats, text messages, and I don't want you or Claude giving each other the cold shoulder. This situation might be awkward, but you're friends first and foremost."

This *is* good news, and I manage a real smile. "Penny, that's awesome. Don't worry, the sting will go away soon, then I'll message Claude and tell him there are no hard feelings. I'll let him worry for a few more days first."

Penny's grin is wicked. "Good. Now, how about a walk, then I'll drive you home? I also took the car so Claude couldn't take Amélie out if she cried too much."

"You're so mean," I say with a laugh, "but a walk does sound lovely. Thank you."

As we leave, I take one last look back at the Eiffel Tower and bid it, and my life in Paris, a silent goodbye.

Chapter 20

Å

Jacques

I did not go to work yesterday. I told Claude I was not feeling well, and I took the day to think. Consider. Contemplate. My so-called privileged life has not been a "privilege" at all. It has been a curse, a cage I have been trapped in. I do not have the basic life skills of someone like Jane. Relationships do not come easily to me. I did not realise this was the case until yesterday unfolded and I lost the woman of my dreams.

Did the fact that she did not want to stay after I told her how I felt mean something? No, I cannot accept that she does not care about me. Although I do not understand how she could change her mind so quickly. She always encouraged me to embrace a new life but is not willing to be a part of it.

It does not make sense. Am I missing something?

When my alarm sounds, I am already awake and staring at the ceiling. I did not sleep well because I am alone. I miss Jane. Even her small apartment.

Pushing the covers back, I get out of bed and hesitantly go about my morning routine. I won't let Claude down again today. Yesterday he sounded abrupt...stressed. I do not like putting him in that situation.

Half an hour later, I am leaving my apartment to go to work. I decide not to drive today. The sun is shining, and I could do with the walk. I open the front door of the apartment building and stumble back when someone drops back with a shriek. I glance down at the familiar form sitting on the ground, my heart racing as those beautiful blue eyes stare up at me.

"Jane," I breathe, so many questions running around my mind. As I help her to her feet, I see a couple of suitcases next to the steps leading into the building. "What are you doing here? Why did you not use the intercom?"

"I was worried you wouldn't answer." Her eyes flick to my face briefly before looking over my shoulder.

"How did you know I would come out the front door? I usually drive to work."

She shrugs one shoulder and finally meets my gaze. "I took the chance you would want to enjoy the sunshine today." She clears her throat. "I had to see you before—" She shakes her head and looks at her feet.

"Before?"

She looks me in the eye and says three words, shattering my world into a million pieces. "I go home," she finishes. "I'm going home, Jack. To Australia."

I cannot move. Cannot breathe. All I can do is stare at her, unblinking, as her words sink in. She is going back to Australia? But why?

"I requested an Uber to pick me up from here," she continues. Then, as if on cue, the Uber stops in front of us and sounds the horn. Jane gestures that she will be a few moments and turns back to me. "I couldn't leave without apologising. For everything that happened yesterday." Her smile is wobbly, and when she reaches up to stroke my cheek, her touch is tentative. "I'm sorry, Jack. What I said and did was unforgivable."

The pain of her leaving hits hard.

"It is not unforgivable," I say with a small smile. "I only want you to trust me when I say you are enough."

An emotion I cannot read flashes across her features. Does she not believe me?

"Jane." I go to rest my hand on hers still touching my cheek, but she whips it back, shaking her head, as she steps back away from me.

"I came to apologise, and I have. Now I need to leave." She is stoic, set in her ways...it is unlike her.

She picks up her suitcases, one in each hand, and takes a step closer to the waiting Uber.

"Why are you leaving?" I ask.

"Ask Claude, he'll tell you." She smiles sadly as she places the suitcases next to the car.

"Is there no chance for us at all?" I sound desperate, but that is because I am. Desperate for Jane not to leave. Desperate for her not to give up on us. We can have something amazing if only she will let us explore it.

There is a small shake of her head, which breaks my heart again. "I want there to be." She speaks so softly I barely hear her over a car driving down the street. "But I can't do long distance. I'm sorry."

No discussion. She made up her mind, and yet again, she does not give me a say. She apologises for doing it, then does it again. Maybe it is better if our relationship does not work. If I know anything about relationships, people must give and take. It is two-way. At this moment, it feels one sided. I want Jane and I to make choices together.

I will demand I have my say this time. "Then we talk about it," I say calmly, even though all I want to do is get on my knees and beg.

She says nothing as the driver comes around and helps her load the luggage.

"This is not just about you, Jane," I try one last time. "It is about *us.*"

She opens the door, hesitates for a second before shaking her head and sliding in, closing the door after her.

The car disappears down the road, and Jane does not glance back. Not once. She has left my life. Again.

Gritting my teeth, I turn to walk to work but stop and change my mind. There is something about Jane's changed attitude that bothers me. It has been since yesterday. She has never been concerned about my money or status or having everything her way. Has never questioned being "good enough." This change was sudden...ever since—

"*Merde!*"

Everything makes sense now. Maman and Papa's visit. Why did I not think of this sooner?

Turning the other direction, I make my way to their building. They always start early, so if I visit now, they will be there. I need to know *exactly* what Maman said to Jane. I saw Maman go over to her. Jane disappeared shortly after Maman left and was not the same afterward.

The updated will would have been signed last night, and I am at peace. I have done the right thing. I am still unsure how I am going to move forward, but I hope in time I will figure it out. When I do, I must set out to prove to Jane that she is wrong.

She *is* good enough.

I arrive at the DuPont high-rise building at eight a.m. High above the others, there is a fancy D on the top. This has practically been a second home to me, yet it always felt foreign. I never knew why. Until now.

It is a façade. There is nothing real or genuine about the DuPonts. How the public sees us, it is an act. I will forever be a DuPont; I cannot change that unless I change my name, which I do not intend to do. I can be a *better* DuPont, though. One who conducts genuine business and treats people fairly. From now on, I will make sure people refer to me as *Jack* DuPont. If I cannot completely remove myself from the family name, I might as well adopt the name Jane gave me.

With a smile in place, I enter through the automatic doors and wave to the men on security. The bank of elevators is busy with people, so I take the stairs. We are high up on the tenth floor, but the stairs are second nature to me. I like the exercise.

When I arrive on the tenth floor, the lovely receptionist greets me with a chirpy, "*Bonjour.*" It is with shame I realise I never learned her name. For so long I was so focused on being a DuPont, on doing everything right in Papa's eyes, that I did not take notice of those who worked under us. It made me no better than my father.

Claude keeps me in check when we are together, but when I am alone, I am influenced by my family.

No more.

I am not that person anymore. I am trying hard to *not* be like my father, and today I can prove it by my actions.

I stop at the reception desk with a smile. "*Bonjour,*" my gaze flicks to her fancy gold badge, "Martha. How are you today?" I continue speaking English and hope she understands me.

Her cheeks turn a rosy red, and she appears surprised that I am talking to her.

"Good morning, Mr. DuPont. I am well, thank you. I trust you are, too?" I need not have worried that she understood me as I pick up a beautiful English accent.

I cringe and shake my head. "Please, Martha, do not call me 'Mr. DuPont.' I am not my father."

My voice is harsher than I intend, and Martha grimaces. She lowers her gaze. "I apologise, sir. I did not mean to offend you."

She will not meet my gaze and appears flustered. I blink at her, then take in my surrounds. The second receptionist is at the printer and keeps looking back at me, skittish and uncertain. A pair of assistants do not make eye contact.

Is this how my family is to these people? Almighty figures who must be obeyed and never talked to like "normal people"? How did I not notice this before? Why am I only seeing this now?

Jane.

One person. One name. One love. Who does not feel good enough and now I am certain I know why. It is why I am here.

But first, I turn to Martha and fix what I can.

"You did not offend me," I say gently, and she smiles in relief. "All I ask is to call me Jacques—" I pause, and I shake my head. "*Non*, call me Jack."

Martha's cheeks are a brighter pink now, but she giggles even though she would be in her fifties. "Did you know Jacques is the French version of Jack?"

"Yes, yes I did." I grin widely. "I hope you all have a *magnifique* day." I wave to everyone, not missing the pleasantly surprised looks and hesitant waves back, then rush to Papa's office. I barge in without knocking.

He is not in a meeting, but Maman is with him. They are annoyed by the interruption, but I do not care.

"You are too late," Papa says in French.

I am happy to speak French, as there is less chance of being misunderstood. "I am not here about that." I stride up to the desk and stop in front of it. "But since we are on the topic, I will reiterate one last time that I do not care if I am in your will or not. I will live my life how I want. I can make my own business decisions, and I will make it a success. You will not tell me otherwise."

Papa harrumphs but says nothing.

I turn to Maman next. "What did you say to Jane?"

She holds her head high and shrugs one shoulder. "I have no idea what you are talking about. I only introduced myself. She is very plain, Jacques, nothing like the beautiful French women with whom we are connected. Whatever do you see in her?"

Her insults only fuel the fire burning deep inside me. A fire that burns only for Jane. Who is worth more than one hundred women of whom my family approves. Those women are all fake and only want a rich husband.

"What did you say to her?" I repeat through clenched teeth. I wish she would not avoid my question.

"Only what any mother would say to protect her son who is taking a dangerous path." Her icy gaze bores through me, but I am not affected. "I told her she is not good enough for you. There, I hope you are satisfied. One day you will thank me."

I clench my hands at my sides and breathe slowly to control my boiling anger.

"No, I am *not* satisfied, and I will never thank you. Jane is worth more to me than this business or the DuPont name. And you will not insult my girlfriend again. I choose who I date, not you." I turn my gaze to Papa and add, "And she is *not* after my money, Papa."

I glance from one to the other, shocked expressions on their faces, and a weight lifts off my shoulders. I should have done this many years ago.

"I am done with this business for good," I add in a calmer voice. "I will always be your son, and I hope we will be civil, but I am living life how I choose."

Papa reacts by banging his fist on the desk, making my heart leap. "If you do not want this business, and you do not want our will, you are no son of ours." Spittle flies out of his mouth as he speaks. A vein twitches in his neck and his face is red. Yet he holds his head high. His eyes are determined.

This is a new side of Papa I have never seen before. Uncontrolled. Angry. This loss of control is what I fear. Brought about by years of suppressed feelings and emotions. I do not ever want to get to this point, and it only heightens my resolve to stay on my new path.

I glance at Maman who, to my surprise, appears uncertain, but she says nothing, only shifts closer to Papa, an unspoken sign that she supports him and not me. Papa had warned me they would disown me if I did not change my mind, yet it still hurts.

"I am sorry, Papa, Maman," I say. "I did not want this, but I respect your decision."

When I leave their office, it is with a lightness in my step but a heaviness in my heart. I am sad that, despite everything, I have lost my family. That was not my goal, but it must be. For now. Time is a natural healer, so I will give them that.

My focus must be on finding a way to win Jane back. I do not know how or when, or even if she will accept. But I will prove to her somehow that she is good enough.

⁂

I t is eight thirty a.m. when I reach Maître Tech, and I arrive with a plan.

I enter the office with a, "*Bonjour*," and everyone, including Francine, greets me just as cheerily. Except there is one voice I do not hear. A sweet, Australian voice that now inhabits my life and dreams.

Not seeing Jane at her desk puts a dampener on the morning. I still do not know what happened, but I expect Claude will tell me. I hope it is not because of Maman or me. I glance at Claude's office, but the door is closed. I look at Francine, noticing she is surprisingly happy. Smiling even, which is rare. Something is different.

An uncomfortable sensation settles in my stomach, and I go to Claude's office, knocking on the door, then opening it. When I step in, closing the door after me, my concern grows. Claude is sitting at his desk, head in hands, looking like he has the world on his shoulders. When he looks up at me, his eyes are bloodshot, and his hair is mussed like he has run a hand through it too many times.

"I hate my job." Claude's hands fall to the desk with a thump. "I don't want to work here anymore."

"What is going on? Jane told me she had to go back to Australia. Why?" I take a seat and lean forward.

"I had to fire her."

Mon Dieu.

When Claude fills me in on everything, I cannot believe what I am hearing. Jane made some silly choices, and I understand Claude's position, but it is an unfortunate situation. It is also very wrong of Francine to put Jane in this position and deny any involvement.

"You were right," Claude says, "I *should* have let Francine go the day you started. You can tell me 'I told you so' if you want to, I won't mind."

I shake my head. "I would not do that, Claude. You made the choice you felt was right, that is very commendable."

"Yeah, but look where it's landed me?" He scoffs and rakes a hand through his hair, making it stand on end. "I'm not cut out for this."

There must be some way to prove Jane's innocence, so I make a mental note to investigate some more.

"Penny's mad at me, too," Claude adds. "Left Amélie with me and took the car, so I couldn't go for a drive when she had her nightly meltdown. I couldn't be annoyed, though. She was a friend to Jane when she needed one, and I appreciate that. God alone knows I was no friend to her yesterday."

I sigh. "Neither was I. She only told me today she was going home."

"Are you two okay?"

I sigh and shake my head, telling him everything.

"Your parents are a piece of work, Jacques." Claude's brow is knitted with worry. "What are you going to do?"

"I am still working it out, but I have some ideas."

"Good, anything I can do to help, count me in." Claude sits forward, looking more animated now. "Now, about this bloody company. The moment our contract is done, I'm going to sell. I only took over because it was left to me, but this isn't what I want to do." He looks at me in earnest. "I often wondered whether you'd be interested in running a business with me. I think we'd work well together."

I stare at Claude for a moment, a slow smile spreading across my face. "That is good news, because I thought the same thing."

"You have?" Claude sits up straighter. "Yes, yes, what a brilliant idea. It will take time, though."

"Yes, it will," I nod, "but there is much to be done. We will need all the time we can get. I also wish to find a way to clear Jane's name."

Claude nods eagerly. "Any chance we'll be in a good position by December?"

"Why December specifically?"

"That is when I am going to Australia with Penny and Amélie. We will be leaving a couple of days before Christmas and will be gone for a month. I am hoping my business will be sold by then and hopefully you and I will have a plan in motion for our business."

Our business. I like the sound of this a lot. Claude is the type of trustworthy and honest person I aim to be. I can trust him with my life and my business. We will work well together.

I think for a moment. "Eight months," I muse, "I think it is possible. We have a roadmap already on how to bring Maître Tech into the modern world, but we may need to make some changes to meet the deadline."

Claude brings up the roadmap on the computer and turns the screen so we can go over it together. For the next hour, we discuss this in detail and make small edits so it is a more achievable goal. I suggest some potential buyers who may be interested in the business, and Claude notes them down to follow up.

Entreprises DuPont is *not* on the list.

When that is done, we agree to go out for dinner tonight so we can discuss our business plans. I feel good about this. Very good.

The fear that has been lingering since Papa first told me about being written out of the will is long gone. Seeing him today, and now with Claude and I making plans, it confirms I do not need them or their money.

Chapter 21

Jane

Eight Months Later

The summer sun burns my pale skin as I dash from the tram to the shade of the tram shelter. In my tote bag, I dig around for my sunscreen and lather it on my face, neck, arms, and legs.

Eight *long* months have passed. Far from easy, but I've survived.

I had a long meeting with Regina when I got home, and she let me keep my job. She's such a godsend. It kept me afloat and helped me plan a future. A *new* future that begins next week. Regina trusts me enough to send me on another assignment interstate. I'm moving to the Gold Coast! Surfers Paradise, more specifically.

This is another six-month contract like my last one, but Regina is aware that when it ends, I'll be finding another job. Queensland is where I want to continue my life. Mum and Dad weren't entirely happy about me moving states at first, but they've come around. Now they're excited to have an excuse to visit.

Yesterday was my last day at the office in Adelaide, and it was a teary goodbye as I farewelled my colleagues.

Once I'm lathered, I pull my hair back into a messy bun, then make my way to the waterfront. As I approach the jetty, I can see the tops of the striped umbrellas at the beach bar. Underneath them are day beds, luxe loungers, and beach booths. Around the edges are free beanbags and picnic tables.

I booked a beach booth for the afternoon as the day has come to see Penny, Claude, and Amélie again. They arrived a week ago and spent Christmas with family, so today is the first chance we've had to catch up. I can't *wait.*

Stopping at the entrance of the beach bar, I check the time on my phone. One forty-five p.m. I told them I'd be here to meet them at two p.m., so I go in and claim my booking, sitting on the bench of the booth while I stare out over the ocean. The sun is high in the sky, thirty-eight degrees and rising. Perfect. The tide was out earlier, but it's starting to come in again. The afternoon sun is shining brightly on the rippling water, reflecting millions of sparkling diamonds.

I couldn't ask for a more perfect day to see my two closest friends. I've missed them terribly. As promised, we've kept in regular contact, but it's never the same from a distance.

The situation with Francine in Paris has never been far from my mind. The guilt weighs on my shoulders. Claude never spoke about it again, so I assumed it just...went away. Whenever we chatted on Zoom, Maître Tech never came up in general. Neither did Jacques.

Ah, Jacques.

Oh, how I miss him. So much so it's like I lost a limb. But I learned to accept life without him because I had to. In the end, I chose to leave, but it will forever be my biggest regret. Hindsight is a bitch, because I realised my mistake the moment I boarded the plane out of Paris. I was such a hypocrite. Turning up to apologise for how I treated him, only to do it *again* when I left.

Ugh. What a sodding fool I am.

Eight months is long enough to learn how to live with the guilt, but not long enough to douse my love for Jacques. Because nothing can. He's the real deal, and I stupidly threw it away.

Regina was right all those months ago. The man drought is real here. She set up blind double dates, but they fell through the two times she tried. I took it as a sign and declined any further part in it.

Besides, I only like Frenchmen. Well, one particular Frenchman.

I'll be thirty-one in a couple of months, guess that means I'm well on the road to becoming the crazy cat lady spinster. Maybe I'll check out the cat adoption shelters when I arrive in Queensland.

Smiling to myself, I stand when it reaches two p.m. and go back to the entrance. As I approach, I spot a couple with a stroller and my heart stutters. I draw closer, realise it's them, and I squeal, do a little jig on the spot, and run up to them.

When Penny spots me, she leaves the stroller with Claude and meets me halfway. We embrace tightly, laughing and crying at finally seeing each other again. I feel an unusually big bump between us, and I pull back with a gasp.

"Oh. My. Gosh!" I cry when I see Penny's baby bump.

"Surprise!" Penny exclaims, and we hug again. "I'm due in February."

"I'm so happy for you!"

Grinning, I take a good look at her as we step back. She looks happy, content...*glowing*. I always thought it was a rumour about pregnant women glowing, something people said to give them a bit of an ego boost. Turns out it's real.

I go over to Claude and embrace him, too. "Claude, it's great to see you. Congrats!"

"Thanks, Jane." His smile is so large, it could meet his ears if he smiled any wider.

I'm so glad these two are still happy. Even Claude doesn't look so stressed. The last few times we chatted online, his skin was taut and the lines around his eyes were more prominent. Today, they're not as noticeable.

"You guys are sickening." I grin at them. "Still blissfully happy with a toddler and a baby on the way."

Penny loops her arm through Claude's and looks up at him in adoration, her other hand rubbing her swollen belly.

"Life is pretty good right now," Penny says with a smile.

Claude nods. "It really is. Now, before I forget, I have something for you." He pulls an envelope out of his shorts pocket and holds it out to me.

"What's this?" I ask, taking it.

"Open it."

I do so and pull out a cheque, which is in euros and is a four-figure amount. "Claude, I can't—"

He holds up a hand. "We got to the bottom of the Francine situation. After a bit of digging, we eventually found the emails you mentioned in the confidential bin." He scratches his head and his brow creases in confusion. "It's funny, it hadn't been emptied for months as it never got full, but the day before it was scheduled to be picked up, Jacques had the idea to check it. We found the emails, I approached Francine, and she caved. She was dismissed the same day, and the rest is history."

Jacques? A shudder ripples down my spine at the thought that he was involved in proving my innocence. He cared enough to help.

"But what's with the cheque?" I ask, pushing Jacques to the far reaches of my mind. He hasn't contacted me, nor I him. Clearly, he was just doing one last favour.

"Your last four weeks of wages," Claude explains. "I had to take the steps I did at the time, you know that, but now that the truth is out and everything is resolved, you're owed that money."

He's looking at me expectantly, as though unsure of my reaction. Honestly, I'm just relieved. A great weight lifts off my shoulders, and I sigh in relief. There's nothing worse than being accused of something you didn't do and have it hanging over your head.

I tuck the cheque into my bag, then hug Claude again, squeezing tight. "Thank you. This means a lot to me."

I don't bother asking why Francine did it. I made my assumptions, but I really don't care if I'm right or not. The fact is what she did was wrong.

"It wasn't just me. Jacques helped, too." His eyes go unnaturally wide when he says this, like he's hinting at something, but I have no idea what.

"Right, well," I rub my nose, "say thanks from me, then."

I draw in a deep breath and release it slowly, feeling a little overwhelmed by everything. I'm justifiably vindicated over the Francine situation, but now everything feels a little awkward. Now that

Jacques has been mentioned, I should say something, ask how he is, *anything*. But I also don't want to know. If I learn he's got a girlfriend, or a fiancée, it will destroy me.

In the end, I realise not asking will be rude. "He's doing well, I hope?"

I'm not sure why Claude laughs, but when he does, he sounds...relieved? "Very well, actually. He says hi."

I roll my eyes and scoff. Of course he says hi. What else would he say? Why would he bother to ask after me, ask if I'm okay, when *I* left him like an idiot?

If I was looking for any sign that he'd given up on me, which I wasn't, by the way, this would be it. He says *hi*? That's a definite hint for "stop moping, you idiot, and forget about him once and for all."

My skin prickles, and I shiver the same moment I hear a voice. "Hi."

I yelp in fright and spin around. That voice. I could never forget it. I hear it in my dreams every night.

Jacques? In...*Glenelg*? He left Paris?

I can't move. Can't speak. All I can do is stare, taking him in from head to toe. His signature coif I desperately want to run my fingers through. Those dark brown eyes, shining in the summer sun, that smile with the dimples...oh, those dimples.

"Wait, this was *your* doing?" I ask, turning to Claude, who's snickering with Penny.

"You're an absolute nightmare, Jane." Claude shakes his head in dismay. "We had this all planned, but trying to get *you* to ask how he is so he can say hi, geez!"

This was a setup. As in Jacques and Claude talked about it. Talked about him coming here to see me. *Me.* Despite everything I did. Not giving him a choice, thinking I knew better. Thinking that because I thought I wasn't good enough, that he'd think the same way.

I should be elated that he's here, willing to give me a second chance. Hell, I should be laughing along with Claude because that's what I'd normally do. Jane doesn't get the joke, ha ha. But I can't laugh. Instead, my bottom lip wobbles and tears sting my eyes. The ball of emotion in my chest is rising swiftly, threatening to choke me.

If I don't put space between us soon, I'm going to be a blubbering mess in front of everyone, which was *not* my plan for today.

"I'm so sorry," I turn back to Jacques, "I just...I need," I swallow a sob, "I need a few minutes."

I go to push past him, but his hand wraps around my arm, stopping me in my tracks.

"*Non*," Jacques pulls me against his chest and wraps his arms around me, "you do not get to run away. Not this time."

His words touch me deep. The fact he still wants me is my undoing. I relax against his chest, and his arms tighten around me protectively as my tears come hard and fast. Being in his arms again, inhaling his familiar scent...I'm home, exactly where I need to be.

I'm vaguely aware of my surroundings. People talking and laughing, kids squealing in the water, seagulls squawking, the soft breeze, a gentle caress against us, the hot sun beating down over us. But most of all, Jacques' embrace, his comfort, his *love* tops it all.

When I manage to pull myself together, I sniffle and pull back. Jacques loosens his grip, but he doesn't let me go. His eyes never move from my face as I wipe my tears away.

"What are you—"

But I'm silenced by him pressing his lips against mine in a kiss that trumps all the others. So familiar, yet different somehow, too. The Australian summer warmth on his lips, the saltiness from the ocean, the *sureness* that this is where he wants to be. Any uncertainty I have washes away. Now all that's left is regret. Regret that I wasted eight months.

"This time *I* do the talking," he says when he pulls away, holding my gaze.

Breathing heavily and too dazed by the kiss, all I can do is nod.

"I am here by choice, Jane. *I* made the decision to join Claude and Penny on their trip. My family disowned me the day after Papa signed the new will, but I am at peace." He lifts my chin with his thumb and index finger, looking deep into my eyes. "If you still want me, I want to be with you more than anything. *Je t'aime.*"

He leans in to kiss me quickly, but softly, proving his point.

"Yes, I want to be with you," I whisper, my heart racing, unable to fully believe this is happening. "I love you, too."

A slow smile stretches across his face. "*Bien*, but we must work together. Our relationship is not just about you, or just about me. It is about *us*. We must always communicate our worries and concerns."

I wince in shame. "I'm sorry, Jack." I meet his gaze when I say this because I don't want him to doubt me. "I'm sorry I didn't let you talk about our choices, and I'm sorry I didn't believe you. Do you forgive me?"

"There is nothing to forgive." His thumb strokes my cheek lovingly. "All I ask is you trust me. I know what Maman said to you, and I apologise, but it is not true. You are good enough, and only *I* can decide that."

"I know that now. She scared me a little, but I will do better at not letting her get to me so much next time."

Jacques rolls his eyes and steps back. "Maman scares a lot of people. I will not be surprised if she scares you again, but so long as you talk to me first, we will work through it—"

"—together," we say in unison.

He smiles and nods, and oh my, this is a new side of Jacques I have never seen. One I like very much. Determined. Sure. *Independent.* He's found his feet and stepped out of the ever-looming shadow of the DuPont name and into the light as himself.

"Come on, you two lovebirds," Claude calls. "We're boiling out here. Jane, you said you'd booked a table or something?"

"*Oui*, please take me out of this horrible heat." Jacques wipes his forehead with the back of his hand. "The sun in this country melts my French skin."

Laughing, I take Jacques' hand and lead him into the beach bar, Claude and Penny following with the stroller. I'm totally and completely happy for the first time in months. We're going to be okay. Now all we have to figure out is *how* we're going to work.

We stop outside a van to order food and drinks. "I've set up a tab so tonight is on me. No arguments. You all helped me so much in Paris, now I'm returning the favour."

I look at all three pointedly, daring them to argue, but they gracefully back down with no more than a mutter of acceptance.

After placing orders for drinks, and food for those who are hungry—Claude mostly—we settle in the booth under the umbrella.

With Jacques' arm across my shoulders, I relax against him and enjoy the soft breeze against my skin. The shade of the umbrella takes the edge off the heat, and it's lovely sitting with friends admiring the sparkling ocean only a few metres in front of us.

Jacques fits naturally in this environment, too. He's even wearing appropriate clothing, probably suggested by Claude. Board shorts, a plain short-sleeve shirt, and sandals on his feet. I don't know designer labels very well, but today Jacques' clothes look normal. This man has come a long way, and I couldn't be prouder.

The afternoon is a blur of food, drinks, sunshine, and swimming. Claude and Jacques tell me all about the sale of Maître Tech and their new business venture together. A direct competitor to Entreprises DuPont is a bold move, but one I know they will pull off well. I'm excited for them, and I love watching them talk about their ideas animatedly. When they start talking about Claude managing things in Paris while Jacques focuses on finding international clients, an idea comes to mind.

Penny leaves to take Amélie to her parents' place but returns to watch the sunset. Now as the sun lowers in the sky, Penny and Claude are on one side of the booth, wrapped in each other's arms, talking. Jacques and I are in the same position on the other side.

Bliss.

The only word I can think of right now. Total and utter bliss.

As the yellow orb of the sun lowers below the horizon, the light clouds turn a stunning orangey-red. People on the beach stop to admire, others taking photos, most watching the spectacular display.

Now is the perfect moment to share my thoughts with Jacques. "So, I've been thinking," I say as I sip my cocktail, comfortable leaning against Jacques' chest.

"Hmm?"

He sounds totally blissed out while he watches the sunset, a content smile on his face.

"About us, and the one thing we haven't talked about."

He gives me his full attention and nods. "Where we live, *oui*, I agree. This is important to discuss. I had an idea, too. What is yours?"

"Six months in Australia, six months in France. We do a trial, a stint in each country, then talk about how it's working."

His eyes light up, and he grins. "I had the same idea. We think the same." He squeezes my shoulder and kisses my temple. "How do you feel about starting the first stint here? Since I am already here, it will not be a problem to stay on. Although," he puffs out a breath and wipes his brow with the back of his free hand, "it will take a while to get used to your extreme heat."

I chuckle. "You will. People usually do. But don't get too used to this heat. I'm going to be moving to Queensland next week for a new job. Then you'll have to acclimatise to the humidity, and that's a completely different kettle of fish."

Jacques stares at me with an amused smile. "You still surprise me with your odd expressions, but I understand what you are saying. I will go wherever you go, Jane."

Then he leans in and seals it with a kiss.

Also in This Series

Troubled in Paradise, the second book in the series continues Jane and Jacques story. Available for preorder now.

https://books2read.com/TroubledinParadise

Other Books by Lisa Stanbridge

Abandoned Hearts is my debut novel. A heartfelt story about two broken individuals who must learn to trust again.

Finally free from her abusive ex, Claire Stone accepts a job as a live-in nurse in the small beach-side town of Busselton, Western Australia. A new life is exactly what she needs. Move away, move on, forget. If only things were that simple. Even the intriguing but abrasive son of her new patient can't shield her from relentless memories.

Michael Karalis is watching his mother die while battling his ex-wife for custody of his five year old son. He's bitter, broken, and distrustful, but Claire becomes a light in his world, despite his reservations. Two broken souls need to learn to trust again and open their hearts or they'll never find the love they both need.

Navigate to the URL below to pre-order this book.

https://books2read.com/AbandonedHearts

Acknowledgments

Thank you for reading **Lonely in Paris**. I hope you enjoyed it.

I visited Paris a few years ago and fell in love. It's not known as The City of Love for nothing. It took my breath away and I wish I could have spent longer than a weekend there. I haven't had a chance to go back, but I hope to make it a reality one day soon!

When the opportunity arose to write a short novel as part of a Paris anthology, I jumped at the opportunity. The story pretty much wrote itself, with a few blips along the way. But Jane and Jacques were always real in my mind and the story came together.

This was meant to be a standalone novel but as I wrote it, the characters came to life and I knew I had to write a second and third book. Book 2 will be released on 16th May 2023 and Book 3 will be released around September 2023 (date to be confirmed).

As always, this story couldn't have been written without the help of so many wonderful people.

First and foremost is my husband Pete. He gives me all the writing time I need, puts up with my constant ramblings, and even reenacts scenes with me when I need to visualise something.

Next is my critique partner, Frances Dall'Alba. We started this critique journey about 10 years ago and now look where we are. Thank you, my friend, for sharing all your indie knowledge with me, and for standing by me and helping me become a better writer.

Then there are my beta readers. Tanya Nellestein, who was instrumental in picking out a couple of major plot issues. Then there was Kim Shepherd, Linda Charles, and Tegan Whalan who all provided honest and helpful feedback that helped to make the story what it is now.

And finally all the people on the indie Facebook groups who were so happy to share their knowledge to help me on this indie journey, and Romance Writers of Australia as a whole, who are always so supportive and offer so much advice.

Thank you all!

About the Author

International award-winning Australian author Lisa Stanbridge has been writing ever since she could string sentences together. As a child, it started off with princesses in castles being rescued by Prince Charming. As a teenager she moved on to angsty teens struggling through life with raging hormones. Now, as a semi-mature adult, she writes sweet contemporary romances and romantic comedies about real people going through real struggles who want their HEA.

She has been shortlisted in many contests, and even won some! Her biggest award is for her debut novel, **Abandoned Hearts**, which won 'Best First Book' in the Koru Award of Excellence, run by Romance Writers of New Zealand.

When she's not writing, Lisa works full time as a Software Tester. She reads anything she can sink her teeth into, and loves binging on TV shows, especially the British ones. Lisa loves lazy days at the beach reading or writing, but rarely swimming, and loves spending time with her husband and her friends.

Say hello to Lisa

Visit her website and subscribe to her newsletter. It will keep you up to date with:

- New releases

- Preorder links

- New cover reveals and excerpts

And lots more!

https://lisastanbridge.wixsite.com/lisastanbridgeauthor

Leave a review

Did you enjoy this book? The best favour you can do for an author is to leave a review. If you'd like to leave one, go to your place of purchase, or search for the book on Goodreads, Amazon, or BookBub and leave a review. Thank you.